THE SQUEAKER

BY

EDGAR WALLACE

British Library Cataloguing-in-Publication Data
A catalogue record for this book is available from the
British Library

Contents

Edgar Wallace 1

Chapter I 5

Chapter II 14

Chapter III. 23

Chapter IV. 29

Chapter V. 34

Chapter VI. 43

Chapter VII 52

Chapter VIII 63

Chapter IX. 71

Chapter X 80

Chapter XI. 89

Chapter XII 94

Chapter XIII 97

Chapter XIV 105

Chapter XV 110

Chapter XVI 125

Chapter XVII. 130

Chapter XVIII 143

Chapter XIX 150

Chapter XX 159

Chapter XXI 167

Chapter XXII 175

Chapter XXIII 184

Chapter XXIV 195

Chapter XXV 204

Chapter XXVI 214

Chapter XXVII 222

Chapter XXVIII 230

Chapter XXIX 234

Chapter XXX 240

Chapter XXXI 252

Chapter XXXII 260

Chapter XXXIII 271

Edgar Wallace

Richard Horatio Edgar Wallace was born in London, England in 1875. He received his early education at St. Peter's School and the Board School, but after a frenetic teens involving a rash engagement and frequently changing employment circumstances, Wallace went into the military. He served in the Royal West Kent Regiment in England and then as part of the Medical Staff Corps stationed in South Africa. However, Wallace disliked army life, finding it too physically testing. Eventually he managed to work his way into the press corps, becoming a war correspondent with the *Daily Mail* in 1898 during the Boer War. It was during this time that Wallace met Rudyard Kipling, a man he greatly admired.

In 1902, Wallace became editor of the *Rand Daily Mail*, earning a handsome salary. However, a dislike of "economising" and a lavish lifestyle saw him constantly in debt. Whilst in the Balkans covering the Russo-Japanese War, Wallace found the inspiration for *The Four Just Men*, published in 1905. This novel is now regarded as the prototype of modern thriller novels. However, by 1908, due to more terrible financial management, Wallace was penniless again, and he and his wife wound up living in a virtual slum in London. A lifeline came in the form of his

Sanders of the River stories, serialized in a magazine of the day, which (despite being seen to contain pro-imperialist and racist overtones today) were highly popular, and sparked two decades of prolific output from Wallace.

Over the rest of his life, Wallace produced some 173 books and wrote 17 plays. These were largely adventure narratives with elements of crime or mystery, and usually combined a bombastic sensationalism with hammy violence. Arguably his best – and certainly his most successful, sparking as it did a semi-successful stint in Hollywood – work is his 1925 novel *The Gaunt Stranger,* later renamed *The Ringer* for the stage.

Wallace died suddenly in Beverly Hills, California in 1932, aged 57. At the time of his death, he had been earning what would today be considered a multi-million pound salary, yet incredibly, was hugely in debt, with no cash to his name. Sadly, he never got to see his most successful work – the 'gorilla picture' script he had earlier helped pen, which just a year after his death became the 1933 classic, *King Kong.*

The Squealer
(UK title: The Squeaker)

by

Edgar Wallace

1927

DEDICATED TO MY OLD COLLEAGUES AT
NORTHCLIFFE HOUSE
Serialised as "The Squealer" in
The Popular Magazine Aug 7-Sep 20, 1925 (4 installments)
and in The Star newspaper, London, Nov 15-Dec 29, 1926
First UK book edition: Hodder & Stoughton, London,
1927
First US book edition: Doubleday, Doran & Co., Garden
City, NY, 1928

CHAPTER I

IT WAS not a night that normal people would choose for a stroll across Putney Common. A night of wind and sleet and a cold that penetrated through soddened gloves. So dark it was, in spite of the lights set at long intervals along the highway, that Larry Graeme was compelled to use his electric torch whenever he came to a crossroad, or he would have stumbled over the curbing.

He was cosy enough in his long rubber coat and galoshes, though his big umbrella was more of a liability than an asset. Eventually, after a gust of wind that almost turned it inside out, he furled it. A little rain in the face was good for the complexion, he told himself humorously.

He glanced at the illuminated dial of his wrist watch. It wanted now a few minutes of the half-hour, and "The Big Fellow" was invariably punctual. Mean, but punctual.

Larry had dealt with "The Big Fellow" before and had sworn never to repeat the experience. He was a driver of hard bargains, but he had the money and reduced risk to a minimum. This time he must pay full price—there were no ifs or buts about the exact value of the Van Rissik diamonds. The newspapers were full of the robbery; the underwriters had catalogued exactly, in figures beyond dispute, just the amount of money that every piece would fetch in the open market. And because of the very bigness of the deal, Larry had inserted the usual code advertisement:

Lost on Putney Common (in the direction of Wimbledon) at 10:30 on Thursday a small yellow handbag containing five letters of no value to anybody but owner.

The "yellow handbag with five letters" was the notification to "The Big Fellow" that jewellery was an offer. A "brown handbag" meant furs, a "white handbag" announced the fact that the advertiser had banknotes which he wished to dispose of. And the "five letters" indicated that the value of the property on offer ran to five figures.

And it was ten-thirty on Thursday night, and Larry was waiting expectantly on the Richmond road. Borne on the wind came the sound of a church clock striking the half hour.

"Punctual!" murmured the watcher.

Far away along the road, two dim lights appeared, drawing wider apart as they came nearer. Suddenly, the headlamps glowed blindingly, and the man waiting on the curb's edge was held in the beam.

The car slowed, the long, rain-streaming bonnet came past him and stopped. From the dark interior of the coupe came a voice, a little harsh, more than a little querulous.

"Well?"

"Evening, boss."

Larry strained his eyes to glimpse the figure inside. He guessed that the timely use of his hand lamp would not only be impolite but useless. "The Big Fellow" would hardly leave his face uncovered. But the hand that rested on the edge of the window was ungloved, and the third finger had a broken nail and a double white scar across the first knuckle—the hand was suddenly snatched away as though its owner were conscious of the scrutiny.

"I gotta deal: good stuff. You've seen the papers?"

"The Van Rissik stuff?"

"You've said it. Worth thirty-two thousand pounds—hundred an' sixty thousand dollars. And all of it easy to market. This Rissik woman put her money into stones—none of that fancy French setting that looks pretty and sells for dirt. I reckon five thousand's the basement price—"

"Twelve hundred," said the voice definitely, "and I'm paying two hundred more than I intended."

Larry breathed heavily through his nose.

"I'm a reasonable man—" he began.

"Have you got the stuff here?"

"I have *not* got the stuff here." By his very emphasis the man in the car knew that he was lying. "And I'll never have the stuff here till you talk business. There's a Jewish gentleman in Maida Vale who's offered me three thousand and would spring another. But I'd rather deal with you—you're safer. See what I mean?"

"I'll spring you to fifteen hundred, and that's my last word," said the occupant of the coupe. "I've got the money here, and you'll be a wise man to take it."

Larry shook his head.

"I'm detaining you," he said politely.

"You'll not deal?"

"We're wasting both our times," said Larry, and almost before the last word was uttered, the car shot forward, and before he could rightly see the number, its dimming red light was vanishing into the storm.

Larry relit the stub of his cigar and went in search of the small car he had left on the common.

"Shylock turns in his grave to-night," was the only comment he made aloud.

Less than a week later, Larry Graeme came out of the Fiesole Restaurant in Oxford Street, and none observing him would imagine that he was anything more than what he appeared, a smart man about town approaching middle age, a connoisseur of good food and the creature comforts of life. The gardenia that he wore in the buttonhole of his dress coat seemed to advertise the buoyancy of his soul; and he had every reason to feel good, for Mrs. Van Rissik's jewels had sold well; and nobody in the wide expanse of London should have been aware of his enterprise, for Larry worked single-handed.

As he stood on the sidewalk, waiting for a taxi, a tall, thick-set man came to his side and took him affectionately by the arm.

"Hullo, Larry!"

The long cone of gray ash on the end of Larry's cigar dropped for no perceptible reason—it was the only evidence of that quick moment of perturbation.

"Hullo, Inspector!" he said, with a genial smile. "Glad to meet you again!"

He really wasn't, but it was a moment for polite exchanges. His quick glance round had revealed the presence of three other gentlemen of Inspector Elford's profession. He accepted his fate philosophically, entered the cab with the three detectives, and smoked and chatted with great calmness till the taxi drove down through the narrow entrance of Scotland Yard and pulled up before Cannon Row police station.

The preliminaries were few. Larry Graeme listened in silence, a slight smile on his dark face, while the charge was read, and then:

"I am living at the Shelton Hotel," said Mr. Graeme. "You might get me a suit of clothes. I shouldn't like to come before the beak got up like a head waiter. And, Elford, is there any chance of seeing this Barrabal I hear so much about? They say he's mustard—and there are one or two people I'd like to make feel sore."

Elford thought there was little chance of seeing that mysterious police officer, but when he had seen the steel door close on Larry, he went across the roadway and found Chief Inspector Barrabal in his room, a pipe clenched between his teeth, his mind completely occupied with certain documents that had come down from the Record Department.

"I've pulled Larry, Mr. Barrabal," said Elford. "He wants to know if you'd like to go across and have a chat with him. I told him that I didn't think you'd want to see him, but you know what these fellows are."

The Chief Inspector leaned back in his chair and frowned.

"Asked for me, did he? I seem to be getting notorious," he complained, and the other man guffawed.

It was the joke of Scotland Yard that Inspector Barrabal, who had been instrumental in bringing to justice so many surprised men, had never appeared in a witness box and was almost unknown, even to the pressmen who specialized in crime, except as a name. For eight years he had sat in the long room on the third floor amid banks of files, examining, checking, and comparing odd little pieces of evidence that were to bring about the undoing of many clever men. It was he who discovered the system of the Dutchman Goom, bigamist and murderer, yet he and Goom had never met face to face. An agony advertisement in a London newspaper, placed side by side with a paragraph in an obscure German sheet, had sent the brothers Laned to penal servitude for life; and they were the most skilful and cautious of all the blackmailing tribes.

"I'll see our friend," he said at last, and went down into the dark cell to interview the disgruntled Larry, a somewhat incongruous figure in his classy clothes and wilting gardenia.

Larry, who had an acquaintance with many policemen, both in England and in America, greeted his visitor with a twisted smile.

"Glad to meet you, Chief," he said briskly. "You've got me with the goods, and I'm giving you no trouble—anyway, there's enough in my trunk at the Shelton Hotel to convict me ten times over. Overconfidence has always been my weakness."

Barrabal did not reply, waiting for the inevitable question. Presently it came.

"Who was the squealer, Chief? I only want to get that and I'll go down with the band playing. I just want to know who was the squealer who squealed!"

Still Barrabal did not speak.

"There are three men it might be"—Larry ticked them off on his fingers—"and I won't mention names. There's the man who bought the stuff, and he's all right. There's Number Two, who's got a down on me, but he's in France. There's

Broken Nail, who offered me fifteen hundred for stuff that's worth twelve thousand, but he couldn't have known me."

"Squeal yourself," suggested Barrabal. "Who is Broken Nail?"

Larry grinned again.

"Squealing's a grand exercise for those who like it," he said. "I'm asking you a silly question—I know it. There never was a 'busy' that gave away a squealer."

He looked expectantly at the police officer, and Barrabal nodded.

"You think one of three receivers has betrayed you," he said. "Tell me their names, and I give you my word that, if you mention the right man, I'll say yes to him."

Larry looked hard at him and shook his head.

"I can't give away two to catch one, Barrabal," he said. "Nobody knows that better than you."

The police officer was stroking his little black moustache thoughtfully.

"I've given you a chance," said Barrabal at last. "Perhaps I'll see you again in the morning, before they take you to the police court. You'll be a wise man if you give me the three names in confidence."

"I'll sleep on it," said Larry.

Barrabal went slowly back to his office, and, unlocking his safe, took out a steel box, which he opened. It contained numerous slips of paper on which were typed, in some cases only a few lines, in others quite long messages. They had all been typed on the same machine, and every one was a "squeal." Somewhere in London was a receiver on the grand scale; a man with his agents in every district, his finger in every illicit pie; and these little strips of paper represented the price that thieves paid who took their loot for sale elsewhere.

He picked up the top sheet: it was the latest of all the squeals.

Larry Graeme took Mrs. Van Rissik's jewels. He went there on the night of her party disguised as an extra waiter. He fenced the stuff with Moropoulous, the Greek, of Brussels, with the exception of a diamond star, which you will find in his trunk at the Shelton Hotel. Moropoulous would not buy the star because of the pink diamonds, which he thought would be recognized. P.S.—The star is in the false bottom of Larry's trunk.

There was no signature. The paper was identical with all the other papers that had ever come to him.

Inspector Barrabal stroked his silky moustache again and looked at the paper through half-closed eyes.

"Squealer," he said softly, "I'm going to get you!"

CHAPTER II

IT WAS two years and six months after Larry Graeme had made his grateful bow to the judge—he had certainly expected more than three years' penal servitude for his offence—and the leaves of the Park trees were assuming their autumnal tints when two people walked slowly along the gravelled path that skirts the road between Marble Arch and Hyde Park Corner. They walked much more slowly than was necessary; for, despite the brightness of the day, the unclouded sky, and the golden sunlight, the wind was in the east and there was a nip of coming winter in the air.

The man was something over forty, just above middle height, and sturdily built. There were long streaks of gray in his black hair, which corrected the first impression given by his smooth, boyish face that he was still in the twenties.

"One has to live," he was saying. "But jobs are not as plentiful as they were before the war. Besides, it's a pretty good position."

Beryl Stedman shook her head.

"It's not the position you should be occupying, Captain Leslie," she said. She hesitated, and went on quickly: "There's one thing that rather puzzles me that I can't understand. I wonder if you'll be hurt if I tell you?"

"Nothing hurts me," he said. "Fire ahead!"

But she found some difficulty in framing the words.

"Frank says you're very unpopular at the office, and I can't understand that—you won't tell him I said so, will you? I know I'm betraying a confidence, but—"

He nodded.

"I am unpopular—dashed unpopular," he said. "In a sense, Miss Stedman, I am an admirable foil to your engaging fiancé."

Though the words were sour, there was no bitterness in his tone, no sneer, no implied self-pity.

"Frank Sutton has a knack of making himself adored. It is rather amusing to watch the almost genuflections with which he is greeted when he arrives every morning—"

"You're not being nice, are you?" she asked.

"I'm not being intentionally unpleasant," he answered quickly. "It is amusing—instructive is a better word. If Frank Sutton asked the staff to work all night for a week on end, I honestly believe they'd pay for the privilege! If I asked them to stay five minutes over their allotted time, there would be a riot!"

He laughed softly to himself.

"There is only one member of the staff who approves of me—a fellow named Tillman, a new clerk we took on a fortnight ago—and I'm not so sure that he is a disinterested admirer. And then there's—"

He stopped suddenly.

15

"You haven't discovered another admirer?" she asked ironically, and he smiled.

"I don't know. Sutton's secretary is quite pleasant to me—I would almost describe her as friendly. Perhaps she's been so long in the service of the admirable Frank that his sweetness has begun to cloy."

"You're being rather horrid now."

"I know I am," and he was so cheerful about it that she was amused.

Somewhere in the world for every woman is a man whom to meet is to understand and to be understood. There is no need for long acquaintance or patient discovery between these two. The act of meeting is the ultimate intimacy; all others are incidental. It is as though two long-sundered parts are reunited.

When John Leslie first met the fiancée of his employer, he had a sense of relief, a vague, relaxing comfort, as though something for which his subconscious self had been seeking was found at long last.

She was very pretty, he was glad to know; rather petite than commanding. Hers was the beauty of violets rather than the boisterous loveliness of wind-tossed daffodils. A quiet beauty with a figure which seemed to him to be most gracious. A gray-eyed girl whose sensitive lips twitched readily in a half smile. He was a little shocked to learn that she was engaged to be married.

A floridly handsome young man, immensely energetic and with the reputation of being something of a live wire, Frank Sutton was both prosperous and personable. His suite in Calford Chambers, if it did not buzz like an industrial hive, was a busy place, for he was an exporter who despised no commission, however small.

Successful men with Sutton's driving force are seldom popular with their employees. Frank Sutton was adored by his staff. It was his cheery smile, the quick chuckle of delight that greeted success and failure alike. It was a tonic even to see the laughter lines creasing about the half-closed eyes, and the grip of his hand transferred a little of his immense vitality to the man who was so greeted.

"Yes ... he is a very interesting man," said John Leslie. The acknowledgment of Mr. Sutton's virtue was hardly whole-hearted, but Beryl saw nothing in this but a reflection of her own attitude of mind.

"I wish he wasn't quite so perfect," she said, and half sighed.

And then she asked unexpectedly:

"Do you know a man named Barrabal, a police officer at Scotland Yard?"

John Leslie nodded.

"I don't know him—nobody knows him very well, but I've heard of him, yes. His name appeared in a case a few weeks ago. Why?"

"Frank was talking about him last night," said Beryl. "He was asking Mr. Friedman if he knew him. Frank has an idea that—"

She hesitated, though only for a second, but the hurry with which she continued told him that she had impinged upon a forbidden topic. "One or two parcels have gone astray from the office. But you know that... Frank thought of calling in Mr. Barrabal. But you know, don't you?"

"I didn't know," said John Leslie carelessly, "but it doesn't strike me as being likely that Barrabal would respond to the call. He's not the kind of man who wastes his time in tracing petty larcenies. He doesn't strike me as being a man who would act as Nemesis to the petty larcenist—talking of Nemesis, here is somebody who is going to be rather annoyed with me."

Directly ahead and walking toward them were two men, both tall, though Lew Friedman's constitutional stoop took away from his inches. A harsh-faced man, with a big nose, a straight, wide mouth and a stubborn jaw, he looked what he was, a battler who had won out. The man by his side, fair-haired, blue-eyed, showed his white teeth in a smile as he caught sight of the two people strolling toward him, but his cheerfulness was in no way reflected on the face of his companion. Lew Friedman's hard brown eyes looked from the girl to her escort.

"I thought you were lunching with Mrs. Morden, Beryl," he said in his gruff way.

"I met Captain Leslie in Oxford Street," she hastened to explain.

"By accident, eh? Good."

It was anything but "good," if his scowl had significance.

"You're not overworked, are you, Leslie?"

"Not very," was the cool reply.

"We overwork nobody in my office," smiled Frank Sutton, who seemed in no wise perturbed to meet his fiancée *tête-à-tête* with his general manager. "Anybody who wants to go for a stroll can jolly well go—eh, Leslie?"

His smiling eyes fixed the girl's.

"And don't you allow old Lew to bully you, Beryl! Lew's romantic: he always imagines that people are trying to run away with his little treasure—eh, Lew?" He nudged the older man with his elbow and laughed.

Lew Friedman was not amused. There was an awkward pause here, until Sutton took his manager by the arm.

"You won't want me any more, Lew, and I'm darned sure you don't want Leslie."

Leslie was trying to catch the girl's eyes, but for some reason she was embarrassed. A few seconds later, he found himself pacing back the way he had come, with a loquacious

19

and altogether cheerful Mr. Sutton laying down the law on the stupidity of old men's prejudices.

"The rum thing is that Lew Friedman likes you—when you're entirely by yourself. But he seems to have an idea that you're a gay Lothario, my boy! I don't even resent the reflection on Beryl, for Friedman has reached the period of suspicion. You can't combat the eccentricities of age."

Leslie had taken a cigarette from a silver case and was pinching it into shape; a little smile trembled at the corner of his rather sensitive mouth.

"You yourself have no objection to my meeting Miss Stedman occasionally?"

It was noticeable that he made no attempt to excuse himself or to insist upon the harmlessness of such meetings, nor did he protest a disinterested regard for the girl who was to be his employer's wife.

Frank Sutton shrugged.

"Good Lord, no!" he said. "I figure it this way: in the past ten years, owing to unfortunate circumstances, you have had very few opportunities of meeting nice women, and I think it will be all for your good. You don't mind my being frank?"

Leslie shook his head.

"You are an experiment—I am always making experiments, and most of them have turned out unfortunate for me. I want to cure you—I won't say 'reform' you, because that sounds priggish. Half measures never appeal to me: I believe in the whole-hog method."

Not even the most sensitive ear could detect any hint of patronage in his tone. He had eliminated all affectation from his enthusiasm.

"Beryl is a nice girl," he went on. "Naturally, I think so; but even if one could stand outside one's self, that is the opinion one would form. I am no pasha who thinks that women should go veiled in the presence of men. A girl can't know too many, as I told Lew, but he's an old-fashioned devil...."

He did most of the talking till they reached Oxford Street, where his car was waiting, and all the way back to the office he was enlarging on his theory.

The offices of Frank Sutton & Company occupied three floors on a corner block near the Middlesex Hospital. It was not a fashionable neighbourhood, but it was a particularly busy one, running, as the thoroughfare did, parallel with Oxford Street. Mr. Sutton, who had established himself in quite a small way six years before, had now a most prosperous export business. He had branches all over the world, a shipping warehouse near the East India Docks, and, unlike most exporters, who confine themselves exclusively to dealing in one product or department of industry, Frank Sutton accounted no business too small or strange.

He was expatiating upon the catholicity of his operations as they paced down the broad corridor out of which led doors leading to the various departments he controlled.

"There's a big chance for you here, Leslie, if you only put spirit into the business—"

And then his tone changed suddenly and he faced the other squarely.

"But you've got to be straight with me, Leslie!"

John Leslie met the blue eyes without any visible embarrassment.

"I don't quite get you," he said.

"I don't quite get *you!*" said Frank quietly. "I'd like to know something more about you than I do. Where you spend your nights, what other little job you're doing besides mine. I'm taking big risks with you. Lew Friedman doesn't know that. You're keeping something from me, and I'd like to know what it is."

Leslie did not answer. For a moment his eyes fell, and then, with a little laugh:

"I thought you knew enough," he drawled: "but as you're so darned curious, I'll tell you my interesting hobby. I buy things cheap and I sell them dear, and I fill in my spare time a with little profitable squealing!"

CHAPTER III

FRANK SUTTON stared at his companion. "You buy things cheap and you sell them dear," he repeated slowly, "and you fill in your time—squealing? That's Greek to me."

"It would be," said John Leslie with a smile. "You haven't had my intensive education!"

And then, as swiftly as he had turned from cheeriness to gravity, Frank reversed the process.

"You're an enigma to me," he said. "I don't think I have ever met your kind before."

"You have missed something," was the cool reply.

"I won't even ask you what 'squealing' means—it sounds like something rather disreputable!"

Leslie was not offended.

"I am disreputable," he confessed; "so disreputable that all my sympathies are with the admirable Mr. Lew Friedman. Now, if I were in your place, Sutton, and you were in mine, I should certainly forbid your seeing Miss Beryl Stedman. I'm not so sure but that, if I were Frank Sutton, I shouldn't hand John Leslie his pay envelope and show him to the door. You're a fool—you don't object to my candour?—to employ me at all, remembering my—er—antecedents. Not one in a thousand rising young merchants would take the risks you're taking in having me in your office, and not one in a million would allow me to meet a nice girl like Beryl Stedman. You're unique!"

Frank chuckled at this, as though he were guiltily conscious of his uniqueness.

"Perhaps I am," he said, and abruptly, as a thought struck him, he asked:

"How's that man Tillman shaping?"

"I don't see much of him—why?" asked Leslie, stopping a few paces from the door of his office.

Frank Sutton fondled his chin thoughtfully.

"I don't know. He's as queer a bird as you. I'm rather suspicious of him, though his credentials were all right. I wish you would let me know what you think."

"If you're suspicious of him, why don't you fire him?" asked Leslie shortly, and Frank Sutton made a little grimace.

"My weakness is humanity. The poor devil wanted a job, and I'd hate to turn him into the street because I don't like his face."

Somebody hailed him from the far end of the corridor, and with a wave of his hand he sprinted up the passage. There came back to the waiting Leslie the gurgle of laughter which was Frank Sutton's very own, and presently he and the man who had greeted him disappeared round the angle of a side passage.

Leslie walked to the door of his office, turned the handle noiselessly, and went in.

It was a comfortably furnished room, its most distinguished feature being a large safe recessed into the wall. In addition to his own desk, there was a smaller writing table, for the general manager shared offices with Frank Sutton's secretary.

That lady was not in the room when Leslie entered—but there was somebody else. Leaning over the desk and evidently conducting a search of the papers was a man. Leslie stood watching the spare figure, a gleam of amusement in his eyes, and then:

"Have you lost anything, Tillman?"

Tillman turned swiftly, and on his lean, brown face was a momentary look of consternation. He was approaching middle age, his hair an iron-gray.

"Yes. I mislaid an account."

Except that his hand strayed to his mouth and that he stroked his little moustache mechanically, he betrayed no sign of embarrassment. His voice was cool, almost insolently so.

"How long have you been in this establishment, Tillman?"

The man looked up at the ceiling as though he were considering the question.

"A month," he said.

Leslie nodded.

"And in that period of time I have found you twice examining my private papers! I don't think we are going to—er—know each other very long, Tillman."

Tillman met his eyes, and the ghost of a smile hovered on his lips. He was the type of man who was never definitely amused.

"I should be sorry to believe that," he said. "In fact, I was hoping, Captain Leslie, that you and I would become better acquainted."

Leslie was examining the papers on his desk, None of them was very important, and the drawers where he kept documents of any moment were locked. He thought it wise to change the subject.

"Has anybody been here?"

Tillman did not look at him. That was another peculiarity of Tillman's: he had a habit of staring out of the window absent-mindedly.

"Yes," he said, "a Mr. Graeme called—Mr. Larry Graeme."

Out of the corner of his eyes he saw the face of Leslie harden.

"Graeme?" said Leslie sharply. "What did he want?"

"I gather he wanted to see you," replied Tillman, still staring out of the window. "In fact, he was rather urgent."

And now for the first time he turned his eyes in Leslie's direction, and again that little smile of his came and vanished. Leslie was perturbed: his straight eyebrows had gathered in an angry frown.

"He said he'd call again to-night about six," Tillman went on, watching the general manager keenly. "From what he said—and he was not at all reticent—I gathered that he had just come out of prison. Did you know him?"

"Slightly," said Leslie. His voice was gruff. Then suddenly he snapped: "What the devil do you mean by putting me through a cross-examination?"

He dismissed Tillman with a jerk of his head, and as the man went slowly to the door, he said:

"Tillman—in case you are not aware of the fact, I have the greatest objection to being spied upon; and the next time I find you taking so keen an interest in my correspondence, I shall take you by the scruff of the neck and kick you out of the office. Is that clear?"

For the fraction of a second, it looked as though Tillman would break the habit of a lifetime and laugh, but his face grew set again.

"That would be a novel experience," he said, and in another instant was gone.

For a minute Leslie scowled after him, but then the humour of the situation became apparent, and he laughed softly.

Sutton's secretary was away that afternoon, and he had the room to himself. Yet for some reason, though there was work enough to do, he could not settle down to his job. Every few minutes, he rose from his desk and walked to the window, examining the street below, and it was not until the dusk came down and the first street lamps were lit that he saw his man. He was not difficult to distinguish, for Mr. Larry Graeme stood under a street lamp, a cigar between his teeth, his hands thrust into his pockets. Again and again Leslie went back to the window. The watcher was still there.

CHAPTER IV

LARRY GRAEME was a single-handed thief, but he was not without friends. He came from Dartmoor on a raw morning in February with the comforting knowledge that the room he had hired in a Southwark lodging—there is a square not a quarter of a mile from Dover Street where very respectable and even moneyed people live—would be intact. Even the great Barrabal did not know of this *pied-à-terre*, or he might have guessed that in a locked box under the bed was cached a respectable sum of money.

Mr. Graeme's landlady was used to his long absences, and since he held what was tantamount to a mortgage on the house (he was a very saving man and had a number of good investments) there was no possibility that his room had been let to another tenant.

She greeted him unemotionally, and he went up to his little apartment to find everything as he had left it. Not so much as a cigar had been taken from the cedar-wood box on the mantelpiece.

He was less concerned about the money in the box than he was about the Smith-Wesson revolver and the box of tightly packed cartridges, for he had come back with one object. Perhaps his incarceration had been unusually irksome: he was getting too old for prison. He had fretted

29

a lot, brooded a lot, in the eighteen hours of the twenty-four when the "lock was on." It was not like Larry to brood, for he was something of a philosopher. The gossip of the laundry had helped to keep the smouldering embers of his resentment red-hot.

There was a man in the prison laundry who had been sent down for ten years on a "squeal." And it was "The Big Fellow" who had done the squealing. Nobody but Larry knew about the broken nail. This precious secret he kept to himself. He wished he hadn't told Barrabal, and had spent moments of agony.

It was a rotten lagging. The "screws"* were a sour lot—he was almost caught twice with tobacco. And all the lags except the man in the laundry were strangers to him.

[* Prison wardens.]

He came to London thinking, thinking, thinking of broken nails and The Squealer and the little Smith-Wesson.

The broken nail was one clue: he had another. The Squealer was a great buyer of stolen motor cars and conducted his negotiations through intermediaries somewhere in Soho. Larry guarded Soho, but it was in a shop in Regent Street, and by the merest accident, that he found the manicurist who was acquainted with the broken finger-nail and the white scar on the knuckle.

"I don't know his name," she said, "but I've seen him going into an office in Mortimer Street—I live off the

Tottenham Court Road and I have to pass the place. It *will* be a curious coincidence if I bring you and your brother together, won't it?"

"It will," said Larry. The "long-lost brother" was the line on which he was working.

This observant manicurist was very vivid. Though Larry had never consciously seen The Squealer, he would have recognized him beyond doubt after she had described him.

He began to haunt the purlieus of Mortimer Street, was a keen observer of people who entered and left Mr. Frank Sutton's office. He even made friends with a clerk or two. The last doubt in his mind was dissipated as he waited in the gathering fog that evening, a small pistol in one coat pocket, and in the other a folder full of railway and steamship tickets that would carry him to the Black Forest Hotel, where he took a rest cure when England was a little too warm to hold him.

The employees were leaving—a straggling line of men and girls came out of the service entrance and disappeared in the murky might.

Just before six, Sutton burst into John Leslie's room, pulling on his gloves, stayed long enough to fire a dozen directions at his manager, and was gone for the night.

Leslie waited till the sound of his footsteps ceased to echo in the corridor, and took another look out of the window. The watcher was no longer visible in the gathering fog.

He unlocked a drawer of his desk, took out a small automatic pistol and slipped it into his hip pocket. Buttoning his overcoat to his chin, he stepped out and locked the door silently.

At the far end of the corridor was an office, apparently deserted, for no light showed through the transom. It had, however, an occupant—Mr. Tillman, standing on a chair, watching through a slit in the fanlight the departure of his immediate chief before he hurried out into the fog after him....

Larry Graeme had moved from his place of observation on the opposite side of the road, and was standing leaning against the facade of the building, when he saw a figure emerge from the gloom of the office buildings and pass him in the fog. Larry dropped his cigar to the ground and went in pursuit.

"Say, you!" he said, and tapped his quarry on the shoulder.

The man turned and peered forward at him.

"Oh, it's you, is it, Graeme? I saw you—"

"You saw me, did you?"

Larry's voice was low; there was something deadly in his tone.

"Now you're going to hear me—while your hearing's good! I've got you right, Squealer, and I'm going to put you where—"

He saw only the red stab of flame, felt for a fraction of a second an acute and exquisite agony, and went to the ground in a heap. Ten minutes later, a policeman found him.

And only Inspector Barrabal knew or guessed whose hand had sent him to his death.

CHAPTER V

MR. JOSHUA COLLIE came into the office of the *Post-Courier* and seated himself with a weary sigh at the desk of the news editor. He was sixty and bald: a placid, cherubic-looking man, who wore a straw hat summer and winter, and had an irritating trick of inserting the buttons, of his fawn-coloured raincoat in their wrong holes. He had the appearance of a retired and benevolent butler; the most eminent judge of physiognomy would have speculated in a wide circle and never reached Mr. Collie's avocation. For there was no crime reporter in London with a more comprehensive knowledge of human ferocities than this angelic man.

He hooked his umbrella on the news editor's basket (to Mr. Field's intense annoyance), felt vaguely from pocket to pocket, until he produced a wilting cigarette, which he lit.

"It was a murder," he said soberly.

The gray-haired Field scowled from under his bushy eyebrows, and his white moustache bristled.

"Did you think it was a wedding?" he demanded.

But Joshua was impervious to sarcasm.

"He was shot twice at close range with an automatic pistol, possibly fitted with a silencer," he continued, unperturbed. "His name is, or was, Larry Graeme, and he was released from Dartmoor last Monday week."

He lit the cigarette for the second time. The news editor was interested.

"Graeme?" he said. "I remember that fellow. He did the Van Rissik burglary."

Joshua nodded, so gravely that it might be thought he was accepting credit for Larry Graeme's achievement.

"And Barrabal thinks he's been squealered," he said.

"Squealered?" Field looked up sharply. "You saw Barrabal? That's a story in itself."

Joshua shook his head.

"I have not seen Barrabal; I have spoken to him on the 'phone. He has given me a hint or two which may be very useful—"

"But what do you mean by 'squealered'? You mean that the man they call The Squealer has done this?"

Again Joshua nodded.

"The man they call The Squealer," he corrected gently. "He is not yet a public character."

He looked very thoughtfully past the news editor and pursed his lips as though he were about to whistle. Looking at him, Mr. Field thought he had never in his life met a man whose appearance was so deceptive. There was something almost childlike about Joshua Collie. You felt, when you saw him standing undecidedly on the edge of the sidewalk, that it was your business to hold him gently by the hand and lead him through the baffling traffic. He was the sort of uncle

35

whom any wholesome boy or girl would have chosen if they had had the range of humanity to pick from. He might even have been an ineffective secretary of a Band of Hope. But in his wildest imaginings no man would dream that at that moment Mr. Collie's mind was picking daintily between three theories as to the reason for a mysterious murder.

"Barrabal is a peculiar man," he said, and shook his head as though in reproof. "He is mysterious, which is against all the traditions of Scotland Yard. They usually tell you all they know, which isn't much, and suppress all they suspect, which isn't worth considering—that is almost an epigram. I find with increasing years my wits grow keener. As David Garrick once remarked to Sir Joshua Reynolds—"

"Let us keep to living criminals," said Mr. Field wearily. "What did Barrabal tell you? Why is he peculiar?"

Joshua felt in his many waistcoat pockets—there were six in all—and found a slip of paper on which he had scrawled a name and address.

"Mr. Barrabal suggested I should interview this gentleman. He also gave me a few interesting facts about him."

Field fixed his glasses and read:

"'Captain John Leslie.' Who is he?"

Joshua took back the slip of paper, folded it, and replaced it in the pocket from which he had taken it, before he answered.

"That is a mystery which it is my earnest desire to solve," he said.

He lit his cigarette for the third time.

"There's a big story going, and I'm scared to death that the *Megaphone* will get it. I have an idea they put their smartest man on to this job three weeks ago. You will remember, Mr. Field, I suggested—"

Mr. Field did not wish to be reminded of any failing on his part.

"There isn't a man on The Street to whom you couldn't give three weeks' start, Joshua," he said encouragingly, and Joshua Collie brightened visibly, for he was susceptible to flattery.

The murder itself, despite its pathetic circumstances, offered, curiously enough, very little scope to a crime reporter. A man, a notorious burglar and international thief, had been shot down in the fog, and it was just as natural that the newspapers should suggest that the crime was the result of some feud, as it was that a fight of East End roughs should be described as "a race-gang riot." Near where the body was found was that peculiar neighbourhood which lies between Tottenham Court Road and Charlotte Street: a quarter favoured by foreigners and not wholly free from undesirable characters. Here are innumerable little clubs, official and unofficial, where peculiar citizens have their dives, and garrets. There were a score of known anarchists living here, and already Scotland Yard had interviewed a dozen desperadoes who had already been in the hands of the police for crimes of violence.

It was a remarkable fact that neither of the two clerks with whom Graeme had made acquaintance had come forward with stories of the search for the broken nail. In all probability they did not associate the victim of the murder with the affable stranger who had been their host.

In such crimes as this, the police very easily reach a dead end. There were no witnesses to the murder, and although two people had heard the muffled explosions which sounded as one, they had not come nearer to investigate. The murderer had walked away unchallenged in the fog, and there was not even the inevitable witness who saw "a tall, dark man" on the scene of the outrage.

* * *

"It must have been awfully near your office, Frank."

Beryl looked up from the newspaper which she was reading at the library table.

Frank nodded.

"Practically on the corner of the building," he said; "and it must have happened soon after I left. The timekeeper says he heard the shot a few seconds after Leslie had gone out of the door."

Lew Friedman, who was sitting in a deep armchair on the opposite side of the fire, jerked up his head at this.

"After Leslie had gone?" he asked quickly.

"The timekeeper was not quite sure whether it was Leslie or the new man Tillman. They left within a few seconds of each other. I myself couldn't have been more than a block away when the shot was fired—I stopped to talk to a man on the stairs—but I heard nothing."

Lew Friedman pursed his thick lips.

"Larry Graeme—the name sounds familiar, but I suppose these fellows take a new one every week. Does anybody in the office know him?"

Frank shook his head.

"Poor devil!" went on Lew, with gruff sympathy. "Very likely he got in bad with one of the gangs and they put him out."

The long library of Hillford, his beautiful house on Wimbledon Common, was a pleasant room to dream in. It was a place of soft lights and panelled walls, for, unlike many self-made men who had come to fortunes, Lew had a nice taste, and he had made Hillford rather a home than a museum for rare furniture and costly gewgaws.

Beryl folded the paper with a little sigh and leaned back in her chair.

"It must be a horrible life," she said, and as Lew's eyebrows rose in an inquiring arch:

"I mean, being a burglar—a thief, and all that sort of thing. The risks they take, the horrible dangers they run—"

"Burglary's clean." Lew's voice was almost sharp, and, as though realizing his overemphasis, he laughed, a little sheepishly. "I mean, it's clean compared with other kinds of graft. I was hearing the other day about a fellow who's made a business out of bigamy—a well-educated man, who has worked every country in the world. A fellow I knew in Pretoria told me all about him; said he'd seen him in Pretoria Central—that's the name of the jail."

"How perfectly horrible!" said Beryl, with a grimace.

"Well—perhaps it isn't as bad as you think." Lew flicked the ash from his cigar into the fire. "This fellow's *modus operandi*—is that the expression?—is to get acquainted with some rich Colonial girl, and, posing as a son of one of the big English houses, proposes marriage, gets all he can lay his hands on, and skips on the wedding day. They say he's a pretty fascinating fellow, and that he never goes after a girl until she's already engaged—"

"Sounds like friend John," said Frank lazily; and, seeing the look in the girl's eyes, he laughed. "I really didn't mean that," he said, "though you'll admit that Leslie is a fascinating beggar."

"Do you suggest he has fascinated me?"

"Now, you two!" growled Lew Friedman, and glanced up at the clock over the mantelpiece. "Time you were gone,

40

young man. Really, for two engaged people, you're the most uninteresting folk I've ever met with!"

He walked with Frank to the door, and under the wide portico, waiting for Sutton's car to arrive, he offered a word of advice.

"I shouldn't make those kind of jokes if I were you, Frank—my little girl is sensitive to certain styles of humour."

"But I swear—" began Frank in protest.

Lew patted him on the shoulder.

"Of course you didn't mean it. But don't joke that way. I understand women better than you, my boy, and the one thing a lover should never do is to give a girl another man to defend."

He waited till the car was gone, then walked back to the library. Beryl was standing before the fireplace, her hands behind her, looking down at the red coals.

"There's nothing to be hurt about, darling," he said, filling the pipe the smoking of which marked the end of his day.

"Frank is crude at times, isn't he?"

"He is a little, but he's decent—and honest." She turned her head at this.

"What do you mean by that? Who isn't honest?"

He paused before he replied, and when he did he spoke slowly.

"John Leslie for one," he said. "I think you ought to know that Leslie served three terms of imprisonment for receiving stolen property."

CHAPTER VI

SHE stared at him wide-eyed, white-faced, incredulous.

"John Leslie an ex-convict?"

He nodded slowly.

"Sit down, Beryl," he said quietly, and she obeyed. "Darling, how long have you and I known each other?"

The unexpectedness of the question for the moment startled her.

"Why, all our lives. I don't remember any other father."

"Do you know—" He had begun to pace up and down the room, his pipe gripped between his teeth, his eyes on the carpet. After a while he stopped before her. "Do you know how you came into my care, kiddie?"

"Why, yes!" she said, surprised. "You were his partner, Uncle Lew, and you took charge of me after he died."

He was looking at her earnestly.

"That's true," he said at last. "Your father and I were partners—we worked together—we robbed the same bank."

She could only gaze at him, open-mouthed, too startled to be articulate.

"That's shocking, isn't it? But it's God's truth! You had to know some time or other, I didn't want you some day to get an idea that you'd like to find out all about your parents, and I made up my mind to tell you. Bill Stedman and I were bank robbers in South Africa. Your mother died of a broken heart when she found that out—the doctors called it something else, but she just didn't have the will to live. She died five years after poor Billy was shot when he and I were smashing the Standard Bank in Port Elizabeth. He was killed; I went down to the Breakwater for five years. When I came out, your mother had been dead a week. She left me a note asking me to look after you; you were just four and a half years old."

She had been stunned, and now she was looking wildly about the handsome apartment, and, as though he read her thoughts, he said quickly:

"Every penny I got honestly, Beryl. I peddled laces in Johannesburg, made a little money racing, and got into Prenner Diamonds—five hundred of them, when they were thirty shillings; bought others on margin when they rose, and cleared two hundred thousand pounds by the time I'd sold out."

"Why—why do you tell me this now?" she asked breathlessly. "And what has this to do with—with John Leslie? Oh, Uncle Lew, I can't believe—"

"Could you believe that I'd ever been a thief, that your father was a burglar?" he asked, and she shook her head silently.

"This kind of thing is incredible, I know. Yet John Leslie is an old lag. Frank took him into his office to give him a chance. He'd been recommended by some prison governor that Frank got acquainted with."

"But he must have been innocent—"

Lew shook his head.

"A man can be convicted once innocently, but not three times," he said, with deadly logic. "Leslie's not a bad lad—I like him, and there's good in him, I'll swear. But, Beryl, I don't want you to get any romantic ideas into your head about John Leslie. Frank's a good fellow, one in a thousand; not so fascinating as Mr. John, but a good fellow; everybody loves him. And I thank God on my bended knees that we ever took that trip to Madeira and met him on the boat."

She said nothing to this: she liked Frank well enough, but for the moment, by some odd trick of mind, she seemed to find her fate affiliated more with this jailbird man than with the handsome young merchant she was to marry.

"On my bended knees, I thank God for that," said Lew, with great earnestness. "I want to see you married and settled with a decent man, beyond any fear that some bright gadabout should ever catch your fancy and break your heart. I've lived for you, Beryl—given up all the things that used to

45

make life attractive for me. I've not even married, though I'll take no credit for that, because I'm bachelor-minded—"

She interrupted him now.

"It's terrible, isn't it—that a man like that—"

He laughed harshly, though not entirely without good humour.

"How like a woman!" he growled. "You're not thinking of your poor father; you're not even thinking of poor old Lew and his five years on the Breakwater. But your mind's on that flibbertigibbet!"

She went red as the truth of the accusation struck her.

"I suppose I am rather a pig," she confessed. And then, quickly: "Does Frank know?"

"About your father and me? No. And he need never know. He knows all about Leslie, of course."

"Of course," she repeated mechanically. "When—how did they come to meet?"

"Frank sent him a letter when he was in prison—in Wandsworth, I think it was—saying that he'd heard he was a smart business man, and asking him if he'd come along when he was released and take charge of a department. Leslie arrived, and Frank tried him out, found he was a very good organizer. When Frank's last manager went wrong—Frank's the unluckiest man in the world with his staff—he put Leslie in the position, and was very generous with him."

46

She had to flog her enthusiasm, and hated herself because she could not feel all that she said.

"I like Frank: you know that, Lew." As often as not she called him by his name without a prefix. "He's a dear, and although I'm not very keen on marriage, I'd as soon marry Frank as any man I've ever met." She hesitated. "I think," she added.

She forced a smile.

"You're very pleased with the thought of my marrying him, aren't you?"

He slipped his arm round her shoulders and pressed her to his side.

"My dear, he's the man I chose for you," he said simply. "I gave Frank his chance, advanced him the money to make his business. There's no secret about that. And I said to myself: 'My boy, if you make good, I've got the wife for you.' And, Beryl, he made good. There isn't a business in London that's made the progress of Frank's in the six years that it's been running. Yes?" This to the servant who had come in.

"There's a gentleman wishes to see you."

"See me, at this time of night?" frowned Lew. "Who is he?"

He took the card from the tray and read it short-sightedly.

"Mr. Joshua Collie, *Post-Courier*. Who the devil is Mr. Joshua Collie of the *Post-Courier?*" he asked wonderingly of the girl.

But she could offer no solution to the mystery of the reporter's visit.

Lew strode out into the hall and found the amiable Mr. Collie contemplating an etching above the hall fireplace with every evidence of interest—indeed, of rapture.

"That is a Zohns, is it not?" he said, in an awe-stricken voice. "What colour! What movement! A veritable master!"

He looked blandly at Mr. Friedman, as though he expected, not only approval, but an exposition of the owner's views.

"Yes, yes," said Lew patiently; "but you haven't come to discuss etchings, have you?"

Mr. Collie's jaw dropped.

"Dear me, no! Of course I haven't! How extraordinary! I forgot everything in the contemplation of that majestic line! I called to ask if you knew, or were in any way acquainted with, a gentleman named—" He scratched his chin, frowned, dug down into his waistcoat pocket, and presently produced a much-folded slip of paper—"Mr. John Leslie."

He had a quick, birdlike trick of moving his gaze from one object to another, and now he looked up so quickly from the paper and met Mr. Friedman's eyes so unexpectedly that the South African was momentarily taken aback.

"I know him—I've met him, that is to say," he corrected himself. "Why?"

"I wonder if you could tell me something about him?" Joshua's voice was gentle; the very droop of his head was a plea.

"I know very little of him. Mr. Sutton, no doubt, will make you acquainted with all he knows. Leslie is Mr. Sutton's manager."

"I knew that," murmured Joshua, emphasizing the pronoun. "After persistent inquiry that fact emerged. Now, as to Mr. Leslie's past?"

"I know nothing about it," said Friedman resentfully. His early training brought him up in arms against the suggestion that he should be manoeuvred into the position of an informer. "Thou shalt not blab" is the oldest and most consistent of the thieves' commandments, and his reformation did not release him from his obligations.

"I'm sorry." Joshua was all apologies. "I thought it possible you might be able to tell me something. Inspector Barrabal, whom I cannot claim as a friend but rather as a vocal acquaintance—that is rather good—thought possibly that you might be able to assist me."

"Barrabal, eh?" said Lew grimly. "That's the fly—the detective who is getting himself talked about just now? You can tell Barrabal, with my compliments, that I know nothing whatever about Leslie, and that if I knew I should not tell him."

"Is it something about Mr. Leslie?"

Beryl was at the door of the library.

"This reporter wants to know something about him." He looked keenly at Joshua. "You're rather old for a reporter, aren't you, Mr.—um—Collie?"

Mr. Collie did not resent the cruelty of the question, but favoured the girl with one of his cherubic smiles.

"Old and artful," he said. "That is one of the great advantages which the years bring—an increase of cunning and a superabundance of artifice!"

"What did you want to know about Mr. Leslie?" challenged Beryl.

"Everything." Joshua made a comprehensive sweep of his hand. It was a gesture embracing the universe, and demanded the breaking of all seals of knowledge. "The truth is," he said, "there has been an unfortunate occurrence in Mortimer Street. A gentleman named Graeme has been found—um—rather the worse for wear. And naturally we are gathering particulars of persons who might be able to assist us in our search for the miscreant or miscreants who perpetrated this foul deed."

Despite the melodrama of his words, his tone was very simple and unexaggerated. He was rather like a child reciting Anthony's gruesome speech above the body of Caesar.

"Is Captain Leslie—? she began, but Lew stopped her with a look.

"We know nothing about Leslie here," he said brusquely, "and you've had your journey for nothing."

"Not entirely for nothing," said Joshua, with a gallant little bow in the direction of the girl. And on this complimentary note he made his exit.

As he walked down the little drive to the common where his cab was waiting, Joshua shook his head and muttered chidingly to himself:

"You have spent fourteen shillings and four-pence on cabs, Joshua! And when you make your return to the office of your expenses, and you put against that fourteen shillings and fourpence the item 'To examining Mr. Lew Friedman's finger nails' you will be severely sat upon, especially when it is learned that the very finger nail you wished to examine on Mr. Lew Friedman's left hand was carefully hidden in a finger stall!"

Joshua got into the cab, poked his head out of the window, and gave the driver instructions.

"Go back by way of Barnes and Hammersmith," he said. "I think I shall save sixpence if you take that route."

CHAPTER VII

THOUGH Joshua Collie and Inspector Barrabal had never met, there was a constant correspondence between them, which had begun as the result of Joshua's masterly handling of the Edmonton murder and the deductions that he formed, which "were of the very greatest service to Scotland Yard," according to one of Mr. Barrabal's amiable letters. Twice Joshua had called upon the inspector and twice had been rebuffed. For Barrabal was the shyest man that had ever walked a beat. It is true he had only walked a beat for two years, after which his peculiar abilities had brought him his promotion to the Record Department of Scotland Yard; but even that experience had not entirely destroyed his natural diffidence.

He sat late one night in his office in New Scotland Yard, and before him was a typewritten minute of six pages which told him all that he already knew about the Graeme murder—indeed, he had made sensible contributions to the minute's contents.

Inspector Elford came in while, with his forehead in his hands, he was perusing for the sixth time this typewritten account.

"I've found Larry's dugout," said Elford. "He has a room in Trinity Square, Borough."

"Did you search it?" asked the other, without looking up.

"There was nothing to search. He'd cleared out everything and had removed his belongings in two suitcases on the day of the murder. Cook's had issued the tickets to Germany, and, as you know, we found the suitcases in the Victoria luggage room."

Barrabal leaned back in his chair, stretched his arms, and yawned.

"What a fool, and what an unusual fool!" he said. "The last man in the world I should have expected to try that feud stuff."

"He was very morose in prison—you read the Governor's report?" asked Elford. "I've seen men like that go that way before. You saw him the night he was arrested, and you saw him again the next morning, didn't you?"

Inspector Barrabal nodded.

"What did he tell you in the morning?"

"Quite a lot of things, but only one of interest." Barrabal was in his usual uncommunicative mood.

Elford stroked his long beard, walked to the window and peered out on to the Embankment.

"I saw the usual yellow envelope, private and confidential, on your desk at eight o'clock when I looked in," he said. "Was it a squeal?"

"A big one," said Barrabal, "and a pretty interesting one, too."

He crossed to the safe, took out a box, and showed his assistant the latest contribution to the sum of the Squealer collection.

"The same portable Remington, the same paper." Elford, a short-sighted man, held the paper under the light of the table lamp.

Three diamond bar brooches, four emerald and diamond rings, seven ear drops (diamond), the proceeds of the robbery at the Berners Street jewellery store, will be transferred to-night. To-morrow I will give you information as to where they can be found.

"Which means," said Barrabal, "that The Squealer has made his bid for the property and so far it hasn't been accepted. He doesn't expect it to be accepted, either, but he's hanging on in case the stuff falls into his hands. If it does, we shall hear no more about it. We've had one or two cases like that, where a recalcitrant thief has changed his mind."

"Where did you get that word 'recalcitrant'?" asked Elford, fascinated.

"In a dictionary," said Barrabal.

He had an hour's work to do before he left the office, and, turning up his coat collar, walked out into the wretched night.

He saw a man standing under a lamp post on the Embankment, and as he turned left to follow the line of the Embankment, the loiterer took one step toward him. Though Barrabal could not see his face, he knew the man was peering at him, and his nose went down till it touched the edge of his upturned collar. It seemed as though the stranger would speak, but evidently he changed his mind and moved abruptly away, though not before Barrabal had recognized him. Looking over his shoulder, he saw the figure walking across the road toward Westminster Bridge, and the detective turned back to the Yard, and had the good fortune to find a detective sergeant leaving Cannon Row police station. Together they hurried across the road, and presently Barrabal saw his man.

"Tail him up," he said laconically. "I want to know where he lives, and exactly what is his real occupation. Report to me by 'phone at my flat at seven-thirty to-morrow morning."

The detective sergeant's task was a comparatively easy one. South of the Thames, the man who had been watching Scotland Yard boarded a tram and, secure in the knowledge that he would not be recognized, the sergeant followed him. At the crossroads at the Elephant and Castle the tram stopped, and with another glance at his quarry the sergeant resumed his study of the evening newspaper. As the tram started he looked up. To his amazement, the man, who had been sitting in a corner near the door, had disappeared.

He was off the car in a moment and looked round. There was no sign of his man, and he cursed aloud. And then, as he stood, hesitating, on the edge of the sidewalk, somebody plucked him by the side, and he looked round into a familiar face.

"Hullo, Collie!" he said, recognizing the reporter, a constant visitor to Scotland Yard. "Did you see—"

"The gentleman you are looking for," said Mr. Collie gently, "has just vanished into the bowels of the earth, like, if I may use the expression, an unquiet spirit. In other words," said Mr. Joshua Collie with relish, "he has taken the Tube."

"Do you know him?" asked the astonished sergeant.

Mr. Collie nodded.

"I am slightly acquainted with him, and in ordinary circumstances I could feel quite friendly toward him. But at the moment he annoys me most intensely."

"Who is he?" asked Sergeant Brown.

Mr. Collie beamed at him, but pretended not to hear.

"How did you know I was 'tailing' him?" asked the exasperated officer.

"Because I was also 'tailing' him," said Mr. Collie calmly. "In fact, I boarded the tramcar very soon after you. I'm surprised that you did not notice me."

He seemed not at all disappointed that his shadowing had ended so unsatisfactorily. He himself descended to the railway platform a few minutes after, glancing anxiously at the big station clock as he entered the train.

Frank Sutton had a secretary, who dined in a restaurant in Haymarket every night and took her supper at a cheaper restaurant in Coventry Street after the picture houses had discharged their audiences, for Miss Millie Trent was a passionate fan. All this, Joshua had discovered by patient and subterranean investigations. It had been his experience that pleasant-faced men of sixty, with a gentle manner, can become acquainted even with strangers much more readily than men who are less favoured in the matters of years and innocent expression. But though he waited until midnight, Miss Trent did not put in an appearance.

* * *

She had been, she told an unappreciative John Leslie, to the first night of a musical comedy. She always chatted as she opened the morning correspondence, and Leslie had acquired the difficult art of listening without hearing.

She was a woman of forty-four, rather pinched of face but pretty, with fine eyes and skin and naturally red hair. She must have been a very vivid, almost beautiful, creature once, Leslie thought: Millie often hinted as much.

"I wonder you don't go out more at nights, Captain Leslie. I never see you up West."

"Eh?" He looked up with a start from his own correspondence.

"I was saying, I wonder you don't go out more at nights. I suppose you're a family man?"

"I've told you a dozen times that I'm not married," said John Leslie shortly, and resumed his examination of the letter in his hand.

"That doesn't stop your being a family man," she said outrageously. "If it's as lonely for a bachelor as it is for a—well, a spinster—I pity you! I've seen every bad film that ever came out of Hollywood this last month, and some I've seen twice. I'd much rather be sitting at home in my little flat with somebody to talk to, or listening to somebody talking."

"Buy a wireless set," he said without looking up, or he might have seen her lips tighten.

"If you think you're the only person that's ever given that advice, you're mistaken," she said, a little acidly. "That's what Mr. Sutton says when I tell him how dreadfully lonely it is in London."

Leslie put down his letter.

"How long have you known Mr. Sutton?" he asked.

She raised her eyes to the ceiling.

"Fourteen years," she said at last. "I was with him in this business, and I was with him when he was managing a dry-goods store in Rio de Janeiro; and of course I was with him before that in Leeds, when his father was alive—old William Sutton."

This was the first time she had ever given the history of her association with the house of Sutton.

"They're a pretty old family, are they? You're very fond of Sutton, aren't you?"

She shrugged her rather shapely shoulders.

"I don't know about 'fond': I like him," she said. "Employers are not human; or, if they are—well, they're not your employers for long, if you're wise."

He smiled at this.

"He's two years older than I: you wouldn't think it. He looks such a kid. And in some ways he is a kid, too: anybody can fool him—he listens to every hard-luck tale that's told him. It must have cost him thousands."

There was a long silence after this, which she broke.

"Do you know Rimington Mansions?—they're off the Harrow Road," she asked. "I've got a new flat on the ground floor. It's rather nice: there are no hall porters to spy on your comings in and goings out."

He raised his eyes now and looked at her.

"That would be very attractive to anybody who would be ashamed to visit you," he said deliberately, and he saw the pink come into her face, and for a moment her eyes blazed with anger.

She covered her fury with an hysterical little giggle.

"You're a queer man," she said, with a slight emphasis on the last word.

A few minutes later, she flounced out of the room, and John Leslie permitted himself the luxury of silent laughter.

Yet he did not dislike Millie Trent. There was something about her that attracted him: a certain rough honesty and straightforwardness which might well cloak innumerable meannesses, though he thought she was obviously sincere.

He hurried through his work, for it was Tuesday, and on Tuesday afternoons Beryl Stedman went to Hyde Park Crescent for a singing lesson, and it was her practice to walk from Marble Arch and across Green Park to Queen Anne's Gate—she might have made for a nearer station, and could well have afforded to forego that little extra piece of exercise, for she played golf almost every day; but of late she had found it a convenient and not unpleasant promenade.

He was waiting among the wind-blown leaves when he saw her come quickly through the gates and cross the road toward him. Her greeting had lost something of its spontaneous gaiety—was almost formal, he thought, and his heart sank.

"Well, was there a terrible row?"

"With Uncle Lew?" She shook her head. "No. He is rather a dear, he never quarrels with me."

"I suppose he mentioned the enormity of my conduct?"

She looked at him oddly.

"He mentioned you," she said. "In fact, he told me quite a number of things about you that I wish I hadn't known."

If she expected him to shake under this unspoken accusation, she was disappointed.

"That sounds very ominous," he said coolly. "What did he tell you?"

She did not answer for a long time, and then there was a break in her voice.

"I wish I'd known—not that it would have made any difference in our friendship. Why did you do it? Why—why on earth did you do it? A man like you!"

"You are now referring to my unfortunate criminal past?" he asked her, in a tone of irony that made her wince.

"I wish you wouldn't talk like that," she said, almost breathlessly. "Uncle Lew said you had been in prison in this country. Is that true?"

He nodded.

"Perfectly true—I have even been in prisons in other countries: in South Africa, for example—tell Lew that," he answered instantly. "And I would ask you to believe that I was

61

not the victim of evil machinations. I myself was responsible for every hour of imprisonment I served."

"Oh!" That was all she said, until they were nearing Hyde Park Corner.

"I'm terribly sorry you are so upset about this, and I feel the worst kind of brute." His voice was softer than she had known it to be. "I should like you to still—trust me. That is asking a lot, I know."

"You mean you're going straight now?" She looked him in the eyes.

"I am going straight now," he agreed, and most unexpectedly she slipped her arm in his. She said nothing, but the pressure of locked arms, the sweet intimacy of that second, took away his breath, and she felt the arm within hers tremble.

"I'm so glad," she breathed, "and—and—I've got something to tell you, John."

Every word was an effort. His heart stood still almost as he anticipated what was coming next.

"I am going to be married—next week," she said. "Isn't it—isn't it *awful?*"

CHAPTER VIII

IF THERE was the faintest shadow of doubt in his mind, John Leslie knew now that he loved this girl, and the knowledge stunned him. What a fool he was! He had known all the time, but had sneered this obvious fact from his mind.

"Married—next week?" he repeated mechanically. "This is rather sudden."

The absurd associations of the phrase made them both laugh.

"Lew wanted it," she said. "He asked me this morning, and of course I—I don't mind. He told me he'd been thinking about this for weeks, and had actually applied for the licence two days ago."

"A special licence?"

She nodded.

"Yes, it will be before the registrar—Frank wanted it in a church—a choral service and reception and all that sort of thing... but Lew said no. Oh, John, he's been so wonderfully good—Uncle Lew, I mean. You don't know what he's done for me."

He saw the tears in her eyes and wondered.

"You mean about the wedding?"

She shook her head impatiently.

"No, I mean about—when I was a child. The care he took of me, the sacrifices he made—"

And then, illogically (and here she was very human):

"You haven't congratulated me."

"I'd noticed that," said John Leslie thoughtfully. "Married! Good God!"

They had crossed into Green Park; her arm was still in his, and she held him tightly.

"I'm sure I shall be happy," she said. "Frank is so good, and he's most sane about—things."

She spoke very rapidly. It seemed to him that she was trying to convince herself.

"Marriages like this so often turn out well... I suppose most of the marriages in the world are like mine. One really doesn't know the man one is marrying until—well, until years after. I should hate to be madly in love with my husband—those things always end disastrously."

"You're talking nonsense," he said, and she shook her head almost pathetically.

"I know I am! John, I feel utterly wretched about the whole affair. I really don't want to be married, but Uncle Lew has set his heart on it. If this were two days ago, I should have told him that I didn't want to be married to anybody. But now—well, I just can't."

"Something he has told you?"

She nodded.

"About yourself, eh? And your past?" He was about to say something further, but checked himself. "I don't think I should worry my little head about the future, Beryl," he said, and he was surprisingly calm. "A week is seven days, and seven days are a lot of days!"

But here she protested.

"My dear, please don't let us deceive ourselves. I'm going to be married—nothing will prevent that, nothing, nothing!"

"Seven days are a lot of days," he repeated, and she drew her arm from his.

"Don't let's talk about it. Look!" She pointed across Birdcage Walk. "There's that funny little man who came down to the house the other night and wanted to know all about you."

"Which funny little man? There are so many in sight," he said lazily.

She pointed out the shabby little man in the fawn overcoat.

"He's a reporter on the *Post-Courier*. I forget his name for the moment."

"Collie," he supplied the information. "Joshua of that ilk. A worthy crime hound!"

"Does he know you?" she asked, in a sudden flutter.

He shook his head.

"I hope not. Collie has no especial interest in minor criminals. They have to be on the grand scale to arouse his enthusiasm. Then, I admit, a bloodhound is a mere Pomeranian lap dog compared with Joshua!"

If Mr. Collie saw them he gave no evidence of recognition. He was apparently so entirely absorbed in his thoughts as he walked along, his shoulders bent, his hands behind him, and his eyes glued to the ground, that not even the imprecations of those pedestrians with whom he collided aroused him from his reverie.

"What does he want to know about me? I had no idea I was an object of interest."

She wasn't sure as to this; she had only heard a few of Collie's questions, and Lew had not discussed them.

He saw her as far as the station and there left her. No further word was spoken about her discovery of his past, and though she wanted to speak to him about his future, she could not summon the courage. While she was waiting for her train, she saw for the first time a phrase with which she was one day to become familiar. On a newspaper bill were the words: "Who is The Squealer?" It was the *Megaphone*, the brightest, if not the most scrupulous, of the morning newspapers, and she bought a copy out of curiosity, never dreaming that The Squealer had any connection with the murder in Mortimer Street.

To her surprise, the story of The Squealer was interwoven with the killing of Larry Graeme. She read until she was arrested by a paragraph which set her heart fluttering.

The police theory (writes our special representative) is that the murder was committed by a dangerous receiver who is known in the underworld as "The Squealer." A squealer is one who betrays his confederates, and there can be no question that for a long time the police have been greatly assisted in the arrest of many criminals, including the deceased man, by information received. The giver of this information is believed to be a fence (receiver of stolen property) who is operating on a vast scale, and is the channel through which most of the proceeds of important robberies leave this country. Although the police have no clue to his identity, they are fairly certain that he is a man who has already undergone terms of penal servitude, both in this country and in South Africa. Scotland Yard has asked the Johannesburg police to supply them with photographs and finger prints of a man who, under many aliases, has committed a series of bigamies, for one of which he was sentenced to two years' imprisonment in Pretoria. The moment these means of identification arrive in this country, not only will this arch-criminal be discovered, but it is thought certain that the murderer of Larry Graeme will be revealed.

South Africa? John Leslie had said he had been in South Africa....

She got out of the train at Wimbledon sick at heart. It was impossible, she told herself, that only two nights before Lew Friedman had revealed a more impossible fact, that her father had been a thief and that her guardian was an ex-convict.

It was after tea, and Lew, who was reading the paper she had brought home, came to the paragraph that had interested her. He went slowly through it, line by line, for he was not a quick reader, and presently he dropped the paper on his lap.

"Did you read about Mr. Squealer?" he asked.

She nodded, dreading what was coming next, but apparently Lew did not see any connection between the paragraph and John Leslie.

"If that's true, and The Squealer's the big bird they say he is, I shouldn't be surprised at anything happening to Barrabal."

"Why Mr. Barrabal?" she asked.

"Because he is in charge of the case, and because, from all accounts, he's the shrewdest man they've ever had at the Yard. It remains to be seen whether Brother Squealer is shrewder."

Lew Friedman had qualities which were peculiar to the prophets of his race. That evening Mr. Barrabal was in his office after a hard day's work, when there arrived for him a modest meal of tea and toast. There was a police canteen available, but he was rather fastidious in the matter of tea, and had this meal sent in from a small restaurant near Scotland Yard.

The messenger brought in the tray and set it on a little table, took off the earthenware cover of the toast dish and poured out the tea. Barrabal stirred the tea automatically and picked up a triangle of toast. Over his head was a powerful light, and in the angle at which he held the hot bread he saw something glitter on its buttered surface and put it down again gently.

A few seconds later, he was on the telephone, talking earnestly to the Westminster Hospital. As the result of that discussion, the tea tray was placed carefully in a cab and rushed across to the hospital laboratory, Barrabal waited in the house surgeon's room, smoking a cigarette, until the chemist came in.

"I've only been able to make a rough test; I can't give you the quantities," he said, "but undoubtedly arsenic is sprinkled on all the toast. We can discover nothing in the tea. I'll be able to give you exact quantities tomorrow."

"That's all I want to know," said Barrabal, and, going back to Scotland Yard, he rang for his secretary. "If anybody asks for me," he said to the astonished girl, "will you kindly tell them that I'm dead? No, better still...."

He sat down and wrote rapidly. The following morning newspapers announced that Chief Inspector Barrabal of

Scotland Yard had been taken ill and had been removed to a nursing home. The paragraph ended:

It is not anticipated that the inspector will be able to return to duty for many weeks. His work in the meantime is being carried on by Inspector Elford.

"And," said Barrabal to the discomfited Elford, "nothing is more certain than that they'll have a go at you—and I shall be terribly surprised if you're alive this day week!"

"Say something cheerful," begged Elford.

CHAPTER IX

NOBODY greatly loved Frank Sutton's manager. He had a flair for organization and a trick of putting his finger on weak spots. As the weak spots were usually men, this did not make for his popularity. But, to do him justice, whatever defects he might have—and his staff detected many—John Leslie was wholly insensitive to the atmosphere that he had created during his brief association with Sutton & Co.

In some mysterious fashion, the rumour had spread that Leslie had a past; probably here was an association of ideas, for a former manager and an assistant manager had left under discreditable circumstances when it was discovered that both of these men had served terms of imprisonment. It was really Frank Sutton's own fault, as Friedman frequently told him.

"My boy, you're full of quixotic fads, and they're going to cost you money. There will come a time when you will realize that it is impossible to reform old lags by giving them new opportunities!"

Frank scratched his head ruefully at this.

"I'm prepared to take chances," he said, "and I'm convinced that one of these days I'll be able to give real help to some poor devil who will appreciate the good luck that has come his way."

71

His experiment with John Leslie was, he told Lew, completely successful.

"He isn't at all beloved by the staff," he said, "but that's his peculiar temperament. He is efficient, hard-working, and in my judgment trustworthy."

To be truthful, Leslie was cordially detested. A most unnatural silence fell upon the clerks' room whenever he entered it, and small office boys were galvanized to activity at the sound of his footsteps.

On the morning when the newspapers announced the sudden illness of Inspector Barrabal, Tillman came a little late to the office—a serious matter for him if the timekeeper had done his duty, for the inspection of the time sheet was a morning practice of the general manager. But the timekeeper was an easy-going man—most of Frank's employees were.

Tillman knocked at the manager's door and went in, for it was part of his job to sort the letters. Miss Trent was at her desk, but Leslie had not yet arrived.

"You're late, Tillman." She looked up sharply, but Mr. Tillman was in no sense perturbed. For a casual engagement, he took many liberties, and his attitude to the woman who might do him so much injury was consistently off-handed.

"Time is a relative term," he said, as he busied himself with the correspondence. "Do you realize that they're paying out on the one o'clock race in China and that last night's supper parties in New York are only just going to bed? Do you know that Oliver Lodge says—"

"I don't want to hear anything about your common friends," said Miss Trent tartly, and Tillman grinned.

"Mr. Grumbleguts is a bit late this morning," he remarked.

She did not resent the vulgarity, but rather offered a tacit support to his implied hostility.

"He's been here—early," she said. "That fellow never goes to bed! Have you ever heard of a man called Barrabal?" She did not look up from the letter she was reading as she asked the question.

Tillman's head came round with a jerk.

"Eh—what?" he asked sharply. "Barrabal? Yes, I've heard of him. Why?"

"He's ill—dying," said Millie Trent.

Tillman smiled to himself. He was a man who enjoyed secret jokes that were beyond the comprehension of ordinary people.

"We'll send him a wreath," he said, the smile still in his eyes. "A great public servant—he will be missed."

"Do you know him?"

She was still reading her letter, and her tone was one of studied carelessness.

"No, I'm not very well acquainted with the police."

There was a step in the passage and a knock at the door. Tillman straightened himself and looked expectantly as the door opened, but it was an office boy with a card, which he took to Millie Trent. She read it.

"Mr. Leslie is not here yet," she said, "but ask the gentleman to come in. I want to see what a reporter looks like."

"A reporter?" Tillman almost snapped the question as the boy left the room.

She picked up the card which she had laid on the table and read: "Mr. Joshua Collie—"

"Collie!"

For the first time since she had known him, Tillman was perturbed, and his long, lined face grew longer.

There was a small apartment leading from the room, where Leslie sometimes interviewed callers, and for this Tillman made with long strides.

"Don't you want to see him?" asked Millie Trent, in amazement.

Before her question was finished, Tillman was gone, and a few seconds later Mr. Joshua Collie was ushered into the room. He bowed toward her shyly, and his very diffidence gave her a feeling of friendliness toward him.

"You want to see Mr. Leslie? He's not in, but he'll be back very soon, I think. Won't you sit down?"

Joshua seated himself carefully.

"I suppose Mr. Sutton is in town?"

Millie informed him that Mr. Sutton was always in town, generally in the office, but he too was absent from the building at that moment. He was a very busy man and could not afford to take the time off that other people took. Apparently he was aware of whom she was speaking.

"A very nice man, Mr. Leslie," said Collie, and he might have been talking to himself. "I have seen him before—I'm not sure where."

Millie's lips curled.

"You don't go about much in society," she said sarcastically, and Joshua shook his head.

"No, I'm afraid I don't. I spend most of my life—this is a lamentable confession—in the unhealthy atmosphere of criminal courts. Crime—um—is my hobby. Some people collect stamps, others Angora rabbits—I collect criminals."

She was interested now, and could very well guess where he had seen Mr. Leslie before.

"I don't know about being a nice man—he's a bit of a pig, if you must know," she said, a little viciously, remembering with some sourness of spirit the many rebuffs to which she had been subjected.

"I'm rather fond of pork," smiled Collie, and chuckled at his feeble jest. "That's a good one, eh? Anyway, if I may be allowed to be personal, he has a very nice taste in stenographers."

She glowed at this crude compliment and returned his smile. Perhaps it was Mr. Collie's experience in those great educational centres he had mentioned which had taught him that the more blatant, the more vulgar a compliment was, the readier was a certain type of woman to swallow it.

"I'm not his secretary, thank God!" she said. "I'm Mr. Sutton's."

Mr. Collie sighed.

"Some men are difficult."

"Leslie's not difficult," said Millie viciously, "he's impossible."

Collie pursed his lips, a characteristic grimace of his.

"I'm sorry to hear that," he said gravely.

She had the impression that at the moment Mr. Leslie's "impossibility" absorbed him to the exclusion of all other considerations.

"You want to see him, do you? You're not a buyer?"

Joshua put his hand in his pocket and took out a small package.

"Only this," he said, and explained: "Hair restorer."

They laughed together.

"You're a journalist?"

Collie shook his head.

"No, a reporter," he said sadly. "I used to be, but I gave up being a journalist when I got a regular job."

She didn't see the joke, but she laughed with him. Suddenly she became very prim.

"I oughtn't to be talking to you: I don't want to see my name in the papers."

Mr. Collie shook his head.

"You won't," he said very softly. "I can assure you, you won't."

"I'd hate to see my name in print," she went on. "I've seen it once and I didn't like it."

She waited for the visitor to ask her the occasion, but apparently his mind was occupied in other directions.

Mr. Collie had many natural gifts, and not least among these was an extraordinarily acute sense of hearing. Whilst he listened, apparently with no mind for anything else, to Millie Trent's voluble dissertation on the inadequacy of the police force, his ears were tuned to quite a different sound.

Just before he had come into the room he had heard the voice of a man, and it was strangely familiar; and then, when he had entered the office, he had found Millie Trent alone—not in itself a suspicious circumstance, for in a place such as this, he could imagine, clerks came and went with bewildering rapidity. As a newspaper man he was by nature suspicious, and the voice he had heard...

Now, as, with a strained expression of attention on his face, he listened to Millie, he heard the faint squeak of a shoe outside the door, the stealthy creak of leather which meant

77

that somebody was moving otherwise noiselessly toward the door. It was half-panelled glass, and there was a light in the corridor outside. Only the faintest hint of a shadow he saw out of the corner of his eyes, and then suddenly he rose.

"Excuse me," he said softly. "I'm rather susceptible to draughts."

Considering his age and the normal leisure of his movements, he went with surprising swiftness to the door, and jerked it open. Tillman was standing there, his head bent, his eyes half closed.

"Excuse me," said Mr. Collie politely. "Are you coming in?"

But Tillman had already turned on his heel and was walking rapidly along the corridor. Mr. Collie closed the door, a holy smile on his face.

"Who was that?" asked Millie. "The door was shut, wasn't it?"

"It is shut now," said Mr. Collie.

"It was Tillman you were talking to, wasn't it? What did he want?"

"Tillman, eh?" Joshua smiled broadly. "Humph!"

"Do you know him too?"

He shook his head.

"It is a presumptuous thing for any man to say that he knows another." He was mildly oracular at times. "I have seen the gentleman. It is possible I may have exchanged a few words with him. Tillman—good gracious!"

Evidently the advent of the mysterious Tillman had produced a most disturbing effect upon Mr. Collie. He blinked rapidly, like a man who has suddenly been confronted with a very bright light.

"Dear me!" he said—he had a most strangely mild vocabulary. "How very remarkable!"

Her curiosity was piqued, and then a thought struck her.

"I see what you mean! He's another of Mr. Sutton's experiments, and you've seen him in the dock at the Old Bailey, too!"

Again Joshua shook his head.

"I have seen him at the Old Bailey," he said, choosing his words with great care, "but not—in the dock! No—he was not in the dock!"

CHAPTER X

HER further question was arrested by the arrival of John Leslie. He came quickly into the room, saw Collie, and stopped dead; then, closing the door behind him, he moved to his desk, and Joshua, rising from his seat, went after him. For a second, they eyed each other, and there was no friendship in Leslie's face.

"Do you want to see me?" he asked shortly.

"Yes, I would like to speak to you."

Leslie looked across at the girl.

"For a few moments," added Joshua, "on a matter of public interest."

It was a curious fact that Leslie did not ask him if the interview was to be a private one: he seemed to take that fact for granted.

"All right, Miss Trent," he said—it was his usual expression of dismissal, and the woman flushed.

John Leslie had a knack of rousing the devil in her. There were moments when she could have murdered him; other times when she found him very tolerable.

"I'm afraid I can't go yet, Mr. Leslie," she said. She was brusque to the point of rudeness. "I've all these letters to read through—"

"Read them somewhere else," said Leslie.

Joshua Collie, an observer, saw that her hands were trembling with rage as she picked up the correspondence and almost ran from the room. Evidently there was no love lost between Mr. Sutton's secretary and Mr. Sutton's energetic general manager. This fact he noted for future guidance, for a definite knowledge of antagonisms is even more useful than an acquaintance with friendships.

He handed his card to Leslie, who glanced at it and dropped it on the table.

"Sit down, Mr. Collie," and, when Joshua accepted the invitation: "Well, why do you want to interview me? I didn't see the murder—I suppose you have come about the murder—I didn't even hear the shots fired, and, generally speaking, I have no information that a reporter would find it worth his while to put in a notebook."

Joshua coughed.

"I have come to see you on rather a delicate matter," he said. "In fact, I don't know that I've ever had to approach a man in circumstances which were more embarrassing to me."

There was a hint of a smile in John Leslie's eyes; some things amused him; possibly one of them was a diffident reporter.

"You can't shock me," he said. "If you think you can—shoot! It isn't about the murder?"

"No," said Joshua, and coughed again. "The fact is, Mr. Leslie, I'm on the track of a story—quite another story, and yet one which may very well be interwoven with the crime we both have in mind. We have had a hint at the office that there is a man in London who is—I will not say a Master Criminal, because that is an expression which does not belong to honest journalism. But there does exist, let us say, a very powerful criminal organization. It is most necessary that I should get on the inside of this affair, because the *Megaphone*, which is an energetic contemporary of ours, has already beaten us on one or two minor points. Our information is that this brilliant criminal—"

"You've been reading sensational novels," interrupted Leslie, with a short laugh.

"I never read fiction," smiled Mr. Joshua Collie, "except the weather reports." He chuckled. "That's a good one?" he suggested.

Leslie looked at the man curiously.

"You don't look like a reporter," he said, and Joshua's smile broadened.

"No reporter ever does," he said. "That is where reporters score over musicians and eminent literary men: they never appear to be what they are."

"Well, why do you come to me?" asked Leslie impatiently. "Do you imagine that I know anything about receivers on a large scale?"

Joshua licked his lips. It was a delicate matter, and now he had come to the most delicate part of his mission. All the time he had been talking to Leslie, he had been puzzling his brains, trying to recall where and how he had seen him before.

Sometimes, when reporters are waiting at the Old Bailey for a murder trial, or some really important cause, little cases come and go without exciting the interest of the waiting scribes; and possibly John Leslie's appearance in the dock had been in these circumstances, and Collie had caught a fleeting glimpse of that hard, smooth-shaven face, and the memory had lingered.

"I will be very frank with you, Mr. Leslie—or is it Captain Leslie?"

"I am quite indifferent," said the other.

"A few days ago I got into touch with Inspector Barrabal," Collie went on, and he saw the man frown. "I wrote to him on this matter, and he wrote back suggesting that I should see you."

"Why me?"

Joshua hesitated; then his victim helped him out.

"He told you I was a convicted person, possibly well acquainted with all that was happening in the underworld?"

"Thank you," said Mr. Collie gratefully.

83

"And that, being perhaps a little above the average of intelligence as compared with other criminals, I should most likely be able to put you on the track of this super-receiver?"

"I'm very much obliged," murmured Collie.

"Well, I can't," said Leslie definitely. "The next time you see Barrabal or talk to him, you can tell him from me—"

"Speak well of the dead," murmured Collie. "He isn't dead, but the newspaper reports are very alarming. Is there any possibility, Captain Leslie, that you could give me the slightest hint that would bring me into touch with The Squealer?"

Leslie shook his head.

"No possibility at all," he said.

Joshua rose.

"I sha'n't see Barrabal, because nobody sees him." He looked round at the door that led to the corridor, gazed at it absently. "At least, nobody of consequence. I'm sorry you're not able to help me. I've got to find somebody who will. In fact, Mr. Leslie, I'm going to comb London till I come up with The Squealer, because I have it in my bones that The Squealer is going to be the biggest story we've printed since Crippen."

He was looking hard at Leslie as he spoke, but the good-looking manager did not flinch.

"You fascinate me," he said drily. "The one thing in the world I should like to do would be to provide your interesting publication with a good story! And the fact that I can't oblige you will certainly keep me awake at nights."

But sarcasm was wasted on Joshua.

"You cannot give me a hint—about The Squealer?"

Leslie put up his hand to hide a yawn.

"The Squealer probably exists only in the fertile imagination of newspaper reporters," he said pointedly, and Joshua inclined his head.

"'Fertile,' I think you said? Thank you! I hope I haven't disturbed you?"

"Nothing disturbs me," said John, as he sat down at his desk and turned over the papers awaiting his attention.

"Good! You've spoiled a very fine clue. My information was that you might be able to put me on the track of your friend—when I say 'your friend' I am speaking figuratively: he is my friend for life if I can make a story out of him."

Leslie looked up.

"Do you dream these things?" he asked.

"I never dream," said Joshua complacently. "I'm a bachelor."

There was a pause.

"They say that The Squealer, when he is out of prison, covers his operations by running what appears to be a genuine business—either as proprietor or manager."

Leslie did not raise his eyes at this, and the reporter waited.

"Did Barrabal tell you that?—He's rather a talkative man, isn't he? Good-morning, Mr.—"

"Collie," said Joshua, with his broadest smile. "Give a dog a bad name and hang him! That's not bad! Good-morning, Captain Leslie."

He walked halfway to the door and turned back.

"You have an interesting staff," he said, speaking more slowly than usual; "and while it is no business of mine, I feel I am justified in passing along a word of advice. You have in your employ a gentleman named Tillman. Heaven forbid that I should say a word against him. But—"

It was then that John Leslie looked up.

"Thank you for the warning—if it is a warning."

For half an hour after the reporter had left, Leslie was dictating to the dictaphone, by the side of his desk, answers to the letters he had received that morning. He was a quick and capable worker, and his terse style and unusual vocabulary enabled him to dispose of the morning's correspondence in a very short time. When he had finished, he unfolded a copy of the *Times* which lay on his table, and glanced through the news. He read and reread the paragraph concerning Inspector Barrabal. It was one of many items in a crowded column.

Nobody knew better than John Leslie that Barrabal at that moment was not only well, but very active. He turned to the front page of the paper and began to search the agony column. Presently his eyes stopped: halfway down was a simple announcement:

"Lost on Wednesday night at 11 o'clock a green and white notecase containing four or five Treasury notes; believed to have been lost halfway down Fitzjohn's Avenue.

He studied this for a long time, and then he folded the paper and replaced it. At eleven o'clock on Wednesday night, somebody would be waiting to dispose of jewels, diamonds and emeralds, worth from four to five figures. There had been a robbery less than a week ago at Roehampton, and diamonds and emeralds had been the picturesque items of the loot. The calendar before him reminded him that it was Wednesday.

He went out to lunch early and was away two hours. He returned to find that Frank Sutton had been asking for him.

"It was nothing very much," explained Millie Trent, unusually gracious. "Only Mr. Sutton has two seats for the big fight at the National Sporting Club, and he wondered whether you would like to go. He may be using the other ticket himself."

"He may use both tickets himself," said Leslie.

But in her present mood she was not to be rebuffed.

"Mr. Sutton says that the fight does not start until some time between nine and ten."

Leslie shook his head.

"Between nine and ten I shall be otherwise engaged," he said pleasantly—for him.

CHAPTER XI

IT WAS just such a night as that on which Larry Graeme had met The Squealer on Putney Common: a night of rain and wind that came roaring up the narrow streets and dislodged slates and roofs on the more exposed part of Hampstead Heath, and broke branches of firm trees.

Fitzjohn's Avenue, that long and plutocratic thoroughfare which leads from St. John's Wood to the Heath, is a stiff hill which motor cars climb noisily. At half-past ten on such a night the Avenue is not a place for loitering. But the occupant of the car that appeared as the clock was striking the half hour was evidently a man of leisure and in no particular hurry.

It moved down the hill close to the sidewalk slowly and silently, the man at the wheel peering through the open window on his left. Presently, he saw his objective, a tall figure that stood in the shadow of one of the little trees planted on the verge of the pavement. There was nobody else in sight, and the driver's foot went more firmly on to the brake pedal. He did not, however, stop: he was moving at a snail's pace when he came abreast of his client.

"Good-evening," said a cheery voice. "I've got a little deal I'd like to do with you—"

Now the man in the car had an uncanny knowledge of the underworld, and knew exactly who was responsible for the Roehampton robbery. It was the Dutch gang, and their intermediary was one Jan Bryel—he had bought property from him before. And this man who now addressed him was English.

"I don't know what you mean," said The Squealer, and as he spoke, very stealthily he lifted from its hook a small, powerful lamp attached by a flex to the dashboard.

"Don't be comic," said the stranger. "You know what I want—"

So far he got, when a blinding flash of light struck him full in the face. One glance the driver gave at the face, and instantly recognized it. Before the startled man could realize what was happening, the car shot forward with a roar. As it did so, three men, who had been hidden behind the low wall fronting one of the houses, leaped from their place of concealment, but too late. Gathering way, the car shot down the hill at sixty miles an hour. Two policemen ran to the centre of the road, flashing their lamps; dodged hardly in time, for the mudguard caught one and sent him flying. Police whistles shrilled behind, and, slowing slightly, the driver sent the machine round a corner into a side street, and that on two wheels....

"Missed him," said Elford ruefully. "Did you get the number, sergeant?"

"I got a number," said the cautious sergeant. "It was a little Panyard car—"

"Little be dashed!" growled Elford. "We ought to have had a tank here."

"Did you ask for one, sir?" asked the unimaginative sergeant. Elford answered him violently.

There was a hasty consultation at the foot of the hill with the local inspector in charge of the party which had been sent to cut off the retreat of the car. The machine had been seen in Avenue Road, had reached the Park, and probably by now was flying through Camden Town. The people at the foot of the hill had seen only a blank number plate. Evidently, the driver, by some simple device, could obliterate that identifying mark, and the police had given up hope of hearing any more of the fugitive when a message came through from the Holloway Road that a car answering the description already circulated had skidded on the tram lines opposite Holloway Prison, had smashed into a lamp standard, and was wrecked. There was nobody on the scene when the collision occurred, but a constable had heard the crash and had made his way to where the wreckage of the car was piled up on the pavement. The driver must have escaped serious injury; at any rate, he was nowhere to be seen.

A police car brought Elford to the spot where, surrounded by a small crowd which not even the inclement weather could disperse, all that remained of the little coupe lay shattered on its side.

"You'll probably find it was stolen," said Barrabal, when Elford got to him by telephone; and his theory afterward proved to be correct. It was a machine that had disappeared from Worcester city nine months before.

Elford conducted a very thorough examination of the interior and made two important discoveries. The first of these was a small, stout, brown envelope, bearing on the flap the name of a London branch of the Midland Bank; and the second, a small folding map of London, on the canvas back of which, and in one corner, was a tiny bookseller's tag. This alone might have furnished a clue, but in addition they found something even more startling. The map had evidently been used as a writing pad by somebody using a hard pencil, and there were distinct markings on the face, which were, however, undecipherable. The map Elford put into the envelope and carried to Scotland Yard, where it was handed to an expert, who an hour later laid before Inspector Barrabal and his assistant a photograph that showed the writing with certain lacunae. It ran:

"Can you see me... park from 3:30 to?... most urgent. J.L."

Barrabal looked from the photograph to Elford.

"J.L.," he said thoughtfully. "Who would you say that was?"

"What's the matter with 'John Leslie'?" asked Elford.

Barrabal stared down at the still wet print.

"Obviously John Leslie," he repeated, "and as obviously addressed to Miss Beryl Stedman. What a brute!"

Curiously enough, he was not thinking of John Leslie at that particular moment.

CHAPTER XII

JOHN LESLIE turned up at the office the next morning with a bandaged left hand, and although Millie Trent waited patiently for some account of an accident, he was not communicative, and when she asked him what had happened to his hand, he snapped, "Nothing!" Later, he unbent so far as to tell her that he had dropped his razor that morning while he was shaving, and that it had fallen on the back of his hand.

Sutton was his usual sympathetic self, but his manager did not invite either confidence or sympathy.

"It's a very curious sort of accident to have happened, isn't it?" suggested Millie.

"What do you mean?" snapped Sutton, and she was silent. For it was a peculiar fact that the only person to whom Frank Sutton denied his geniality was his secretary. There were times when his treatment of her out-Leslied Leslie. He would be brusque, even violent, in the presence of third persons; and that she accepted his admonitions meekly was not the least remarkable circumstance.

That day, Leslie was almost amiable to the staff, and there was reason: he was lunching with Beryl Stedman, and there was something rather more clandestine in this meeting than there had been in any other.

94

"I hate myself for doing it, but I told Lew a deliberate lie," she said ruefully, as they passed through the swing doors of a Piccadilly restaurant.

"I suppose I should also be hating myself for deceiving my noble employer—" he began, but the look of pain in her eyes stopped him. "I'm sorry." He was almost humble. "Why I should sneer at Sutton to you, heaven knows!"

She thought she also knew, but she did not advance an explanation.

He ate very little and seemed uneasy. She thought the wound was paining him, but he assured her hastily that this was not the case.

"You're different to-day. Is anything really worrying you?"

It took him a long time to reply to this.

"Yes. You're worrying me—you and the marriage."

She tried, a little clumsily she thought, to turn the conversation into another channel. Her heart was beating a little faster, for she knew instinctively what was coming.

"I'm not going to let you marry Frank Sutton," he said. He spoke distinctly and emphatically.

"My dear John!" She shook her head helplessly. "How absurd to talk—you mustn't."

"You cannot marry Frank Sutton, however admirable a man he may be, however suitable a husband."

He was in deadly earnest; there was a look in his eyes that she had never seen before.

"But—why?"

He opened his mouth to speak, but the words would not come. He was panic-stricken as he realized the stake for which he was playing.

"Quite a variety of reasons." He tried to lighten his tone, to water down the drama to a state of comedy. "You're too good for any man."

But she did not smile at this, nor follow the new drift he was trying to impose upon the conversation.

"Why?"

He was terrified lest he had frightened her—more fearful that she might doubt his sincerity. Between the two fears, he was held tongue-tied.

"You don't like the idea of my marrying?"

"Anybody!" he blurted. "If it were not Frank Sutton— and God knows I don't want you to marry him—if, by every test, he was the most suitable man in the world, I would not give you up!"

He saw the colour come and go at his speech, saw her mute lips shape as she silently repeated the words.

"I love you," he said.

At that moment something made him turn his head. Lew Friedman was towering almost above him, and in his eyes was a look of cold fury.

CHAPTER XIII

LESLIE was coolness itself; not a muscle of his face moved under that hateful glare.

"Won't you sit down?" he asked in a conversational tone. "Are you by yourself?"

Lew Friedman did not reply. He jerked out a chair from the table and sat down.

"We are nearing the sweets: shall I order you something?"

"I want nothing," said the man harshly, "except a little talk with you."

He did not seem to be able to bring himself to look at the girl, but when he did there was such a look of reproach in his brown eyes that she was near to tears.

"I'm so sorry, Uncle Lew " she began.

"It's all right, my dear." He patted her hand. "The yarn you told me was a permissible lie. You wanted to meet this— gentleman, and naturally you didn't wish to tell me. Let's forget it."

The next five minutes were a discomfort and a strain for two people. Leslie ate a meringue and showed no great haste. He even chatted lightly upon wholly unimportant topics. As for Beryl, she sat rigid and tense, waiting for the outburst that she knew was inevitable. At last Leslie was finished, and as though she awaited such a signal, Beryl rose quickly and held out her hand. Then she turned to Lew and, taking him by the arm, led him a little apart.

"You're not going to be very—unpleasant? I am altogether to blame—it was my idea."

He patted her shoulder.

"I'm going to be very pleasant—don't worry, my dear. When I first saw you together, I felt like starting a rough-house, but that cold devil is wiser than me. There will be no fuss."

He did not escort her to the door, but waited until she was out of sight, then he drew his chair round so that he faced John Leslie.

"Now, young fellow, I've got a few words to say to you."

Leslie leaned back in his chair, patted his lips daintily with the serviette, and lighted a cigarette.

"The fewer the better, if they are to be in that tone," he said. "I am rather touchy in the matter of inflections."

Lew set his lips tight as though to inhibit the retort that arose.

"You know my niece is engaged to be married to a decent—honest—clean—man?" He emphasized every adjective.

"I heard something about it," said Leslie. "But I would rather you didn't lay stress upon his cleanness or his decency—they imply a reproach, and a contrast that is offensive to me."

Lew Friedman smothered an explosive outburst.

"You know she's engaged to be married. That's enough for you, isn't it? You know that?"

Leslie nodded.

"And you know also that she's fond of you—I am not making any bones about it, I'm telling you straight out, as man to man! She's fond of you, and for two cents she'd throw away a life's happiness, all that I've planned for her, and follow you to hell!"

Leslie shook his head slowly.

"I wish you meant that."

"If you don't know it, you're a fool!" flamed Lew Friedman. "And I'm telling you something, Leslie—sooner than see her life blackened by marrying the kind of man you are, I'd shoot you on your feet! That's not a bit of wild talk, it's gospel truth. And if you by chance persuaded my girl to give up Frank and throw in her lot with you, I'd follow you to the end of the world and get you. Do you think that's hot air?"

Leslie flicked off the ash of his cigarette and laughed softly.

"I think you're very much in earnest, and I admire you for it. Possibly I might do the same with Frank Sutton—if I thought he was going to make her unhappy."

Lew was peering into his face as though he were trying to read the thoughts of the man sitting opposite him.

"Now, see here, Leslie, I'm going to be square with you. I want you to leave Sutton's employ and go abroad, and I want you to leave to-day! I'll give you two thousand pounds—enough to start you fresh. I know all about you, Leslie—you're an old lag, and I'm going to tell you what I've told the girl. I've done my bit of time too! I know the kind of life you're living, because I've lived it, and I'd sooner see you and her dead before I allowed my girl's heart to break as her mother's broke before her. I like you, Leslie—I'll be candid with you. You're a man, and, I'm hoping, a decent man. And I know I'm not going to appeal to you in vain. I'll give you a check right now. The banks aren't closed until three. You can get out of England to-night—"

Captain John Leslie shook his head.

"Nothing doing," he said quickly. "No money will get me out of England, and for a very excellent reason. I'll make a bargain with you." He leaned across the table. "I'll promise you that I won't attempt to see Beryl until the eve of her marriage. When will that be?"

"She's to be married next Tuesday," said Friedman, after a moment's thought.

"Good!" nodded the other. "Will you allow me to call on Monday night at Hillford?"

Lew Friedman hesitated.

"Yes," he said at last. That he did not impose conditions was a circumstance which should have made a man of Leslie's experience a little suspicious.

"As to your two thousand pounds, keep it, Friedman. You're a good fellow. I've met a lot of good Jews, but you're the best. Keep to your part of the bargain and I'll keep to mine. I'll not see Beryl until Monday night."

He had hardly left the restaurant before Friedman was on the telephone to Frank Sutton, and for ten minutes the two men were talking. After a conversation that was entirely satisfactory to Lew, he had his car summoned and drove back to Wimbledon.

Beryl was in her room when he arrived, but came down to tea, a little apprehensively. Whatever doubts she had as to Lew Friedman's attitude and the result of his talk were dispelled by his almost jovial greeting.

"Really, Beryl, you're a naughty little girl," he said, as he poured out the tea. It was one of his fads that he alone had the secret of tea-making. "And as to your little tarradiddle—I'm ashamed of you!"

Before she could express her penitence he went on:

"Had a talk with that young feller-me-lad—I like Leslie, Beryl: there's something about him that appeals to me in spite of his rotten past. I don't for one moment imagine that Frank is going to reform him, but if ever I had to take in hand a job of making a crook straight, I think I'd start on Leslie."

She winced at this: the one thing she did not wish to think about was John Leslie's discreditable history.

"Were you terribly offensive to him?" she asked, as she sipped her tea.

"I was extremely nice," he chuckled. "In fact, I offered him a couple of thousand pounds to start a little hell of his own. But he wouldn't take it."

Her heart leaped at this.

"What did you want him to do—for the money, I mean?"

He put down his cup, wiped his lips with his handkerchief before he answered.

"I wanted him to leave the country and give you and Frank a chance of settling down."

A long silence.

"He wouldn't take the money. He not only wouldn't take the money, but he wouldn't do anything I wanted him to do, except that he promised he would not write to you or see you until next Monday night—in fact, till the eve of your wedding."

She always knew when he had something difficult to say: he invariably raised his voice, and he was speaking loudly now.

"*To-morrow* is the eve of your wedding, Beryl—I want you to marry Frank on Saturday morning."

He saw the red fade from her face, saw the almost hysterical shake of her head, and went on quickly.

"You know how I feel about this thing, Beryl—well, I want it over and done with. I've been talking to Frank on the 'phone, and he was just as reluctant as you are to put on the date, because he'd made all his arrangements to leave on Tuesday. But he's in the position that he can leave his business just when he darn well pleases. You're going to do this for me, Beryl?"

"The day after to-morrow?"

He nodded, his eyes never leaving her face. He could read the struggle that was going on in her heart, and when presently she said, "Yes," he heaved a sigh of relief.

"It will be better for Leslie too—I mean, if he seriously likes you, let him know that the thing is over and done with. It will be easier for you, easier for him." He patted her arm gently.

"Perhaps you're right," she said mechanically, and went up to her room.

What should she do? Should she telephone to John Leslie? And if she telephoned, what could she say, and what could she do? She was not being married against her will; not even marrying a man she detested. She liked Frank Sutton as much as she liked any man—except that dark, dour manager

103

of his. He loved her—he had told her so. And she dared not tell herself the truth, dared not even speculate upon her own feelings or probe and examine her own heart. She set her teeth to the inevitable and found the prospect bleak and heartaching.

She heard Frank's car arrive, but it was a long time before she went down to the library to greet him. As she turned the handle of the door, she heard Lew's voice.

Mr. Friedman was a great reader of newspapers, and had a habit, which is not uncommon to humanity, of passing on all he had read as first-hand information such as he himself might have acquired by patient searching:

"...the police think it was The Squealer's car. It must have skidded on the tram lines when it was going at a devil of a pace, and it's a wonder to me that the fellow wasn't killed. The police think he must have injured himself somewhere, and they're making inquiries at the hospitals... blood on the broken glass. Cut his hand, most likely."

She stood frozen stiff, the door handle in her hand; for at that moment she recalled John Leslie's injured hand!

CHAPTER XIV

A SHREWD observer, Lew Friedman saw her agitation, but found an explanation that satisfied himself.

"Come in, my dear. Frank wants to see you."

Frank was a little perturbed, she thought, and after her guardian had disappeared with unseemly haste, he seemed to find a difficulty in giving expression to the cause of his unease. She suspected (unfairly, as it proved) that Lew had told him about her luncheon.

Once or twice he went out of the room, either because he heard, or imagined he heard, the telephone. He was expecting, he said, an important call.

"Let's walk in the garden, shall we?" he said awkwardly, after they had exchanged so many commonplaces that she could have screamed.

Behind the house was a broad stone terrace, and along this they paced.

"How does this change of plan affect you, Beryl?" he said at last. "I'm rather worried about it."

"Why?" she asked.

He looked at her quickly, wondering whether she was being sarcastic. He had never been quite sure of the girl, though he had known her for five or six years. Their very courtship had proceeded along unnaturally restricted lines.

It had been (he had told Lew just before she came into the room) a "slow drift to matrimony."

"I'll be honest with you, Beryl, dear. You and I like each other awfully, I know. So far as I'm concerned, I love you very dearly, and the day I am married to you will be the happiest in my life. But I am not a fool: I know you're not frantically keen on marriage, and I realize that Lew's suggestion must have been a great shock to you. It is a whim of his—I've tried to talk him out of it, and I can't imagine why on earth he wants the ceremony put forward."

Evidently Lew had not spoken of John Leslie, and for this she was thankful.

"I'd made all my plans to go away on Tuesday, and although that is a very little matter, I shall have to work hard to get things settled up. It makes it all the more difficult because Lew, for some reason, doesn't want me to tell anybody at the office when the marriage is taking place. I want you to tell me frankly what you think about it."

She had thought a great deal but had reached no conclusion that could help him or her.

"I have agreed," she said—it seemed a feeble thing to say to an eager lover, but for the life of her she could think of nothing else.

He took her arm in his; and such had been the curious course of their courtship that even this little act of familiarity made her feel uncomfortable. Perhaps he sensed this, for presently he removed his arm.

"I thought we had best go to Scotland. I know rather a nice hotel in the Highlands, and, in fact, I have booked a suite as from next Tuesday."

Here was another strange fact: she realized for the first time, with a sense of consternation, that they had never discussed their honeymoon. She had to force herself to take an interest

"Scotland is as good as anywhere else," she said, and her reply reduced him to silence.

Up and down the flagged walk they paced, not a word passing between them, until he spoke.

"Lew has been most awfully generous. He is making a very nice settlement on you, and he's giving me a check for twenty thousand pounds to enlarge the business. If I followed my own inclinations, I would make Saturday a great joy day and distribute the whole of that money among the staff. I'll bet poor old Leslie could do with his share."

He laughed at this, but his good-humour found no echo in her heart, and she was glad when she heard Lew's voice chiding her for remaining in the open on such a cold afternoon.

Frank did not stay to dinner, for which she was devoutly thankful, and as soon as she could she went up to her room, opened her little writing bureau, and began a letter to John

Leslie. But, try as she did, she could not find the words she wanted, and after a fourth attempt she came down to join Mr. Friedman in the library.

She wanted her mind to be settled on one point, and at the first opportunity he gave her she asked:

"Did you tell Frank about Mr. Leslie?"

He took off his glasses and put down his paper on his knees.

"Yes; I told him as much as I thought he ought to know—namely, that Leslie had agreed not to see you until the eve of your wedding."

"Did he ask why?"

"No," said Lew Friedman. "He doesn't know why I have such an objection to your friendship with John Leslie, and it wasn't a moment to discuss the matter."

She was a little bewildered by his reply.

"Frank said he couldn't understand why you did not want anybody in the office to know when I was to be married."

Lew smiled at this.

"Then he's a bigger fool than I thought he was," he said good-humouredly, and on this unsatisfactory note the discussion ceased.

As she came out into the hall, the footman was at the door, talking to a telegraph boy. He turned as he heard her close the library door.

"Here's a wire for Mr. Sutton," he said. "Will you take it, miss?"

Her first inclination was to send the wire in to Lew, but she took the envelope and tore it open. Perhaps this was the telephone message he had been expecting.

SUITE RESERVED FOR JACKSONS. PACIFIC.

She carried the message in to Lew, who read it and shook his head.

"Probably some reservation Frank has been taking—for one of his clients, I expect. I'll telephone it through to his office."

She went upstairs and forgot Jackson, Frank, and his business—everything, in a vain fifth attempt to write to John Leslie.

CHAPTER XV

THE *Megaphone* was a very bright newspaper with a very bright staff, and its proprietor was perhaps the brightest star in the journalistic constellation. He himself admitted as much with great frequency. If his newspaper had a failing, it was a certain lack of stamina. It would appear on Monday morning with a great world-shaking announcement, and on Tuesday morning that particular event which had swollen its headlines would be forgotten, and another and greater world-shaking announcement would take its place, generally about something entirely different from the "splash" of the previous day.

But it was very consistent in regard to The Squealer. Here was a story not to be dropped, and scarcely a day passed but some ingenious speculation as to The Squealer, the extent and profits of his business, and his enormous wealth appeared in its scintillating columns.

The only man who was really annoyed by this consistency was Mr. Field, of the *Post-Courier*.

"They're beating us, Collie," he said awfully the next morning. "They're making you and the *Post-Courier* look as lively as a piece of frozen cheese."

Mr. Collie sighed, searched furtively in his pockets for a cigarette and, being unsuccessful, picked up a packet from the news editor's table and helped himself.

"Frozen cheese—" he began.

"Don't be literal," snapped Field. "Go down to Scotland Yard and insist upon seeing Barrabal."

Mr. Collie sighed.

"He always insists upon not being interviewed, and if I insist upon going into his room, they'll insist upon throwing me out. Sparring with earthquakes seems a futile proceeding."

"The *Megaphone* says " began Field, reaching for a paper, and Mr. Collie closed his eyes patiently.

"I'm surprised that you read such a newspaper," he said. "It sets such a bad example to the young reporters."

"Do you know the Leopards Club?" asked Field, apropos of nothing, and Mr. Collie looked at him sharply.

"I not only know it, but I am an honorary member," he said. "The company is bad but the beer is good. Why do you ask?"

Field had to think a long time before he discovered the propulsive thought that had fired this random bullet.

"Oh, yes—somebody was saying at the Press Club that the Leopards was the lowest haunt in London. I was wondering whether that wouldn't be a good covert to draw."

"Hunting terms," murmured Mr. Collie, "indicating the fact that the speaker moves in the best country circles. I've already drawn that covert, and though I've seen and started many foxes, Mr. Field, I have not yet got the fox I want. I am not so sure it is a fox. Nothing is quite so disconcerting as to look for a fox and find a tiger."

"Look for Barrabal," suggested Mr. Field.

But Collie did not attempt to interview Mr. Barrabal. Rather, he bent his steps in the direction of Frank Sutton's office. He wanted very badly to see the saturnine Tillman, and why he preferred an interview with Tillman to one with Mr. Barrabal will be revealed.

On one point Joshua Collie was convinced—Barrabal could not tell him what Tillman did not know.

The star reporter of the *Post-Courier* could not, had he foreseen all the circumstances, have arrived in Mr. Frank Sutton's office at a more vital moment.

* * *

There were times when Miss Millicent Trent was a little difficult to endure. John Leslie saw, when he arrived at the office in the morning, that something had upset this pretty shrew, that she was in her sourest mood, as the junior clerks and office boys discovered. Usually, she kept her displays of bad temper for subordinates, and seldom willingly provoked the general manager; but this morning he had hardly got into the office before she sneered:

"You haven't got your pretty bandage on this morning, Captain Leslie."

He looked down at his hand: a thin red scar ran across the back.

"My pretty bandage isn't necessary this morning," he said, almost flippantly, and it was like him to be in a good mood when she was the reverse. "Iodine and wholesome flesh have done the trick. Do you want the keys of the safe?"

Usually she came to him in the morning to get the keys for certain books that she used. To his surprise she said, "No."

For a long time, they worked in silence, at separate tables, each engrossed in thoughts that had nothing to do with the letters and invoices they were examining. Then, unexpectedly:

"Are you going to the wedding?" she asked.

He looked up at this.

"Which wedding? Oh, you mean Sutton's? I don't think so."

"Have you been invited?" she asked.

There was something of malice in her tone, and he looked at her more closely. Most women when they are in a bad temper are not pleasant to look upon, but Millie Trent was one of those unusual creatures to whom a flame of anger

113

lent a certain impish attraction. She was pretty enough even in repose: she could look almost beautiful under the stress of strong emotions.

"You're quite radiant with wrath this morning. What is the matter?" he bantered her.

"It's worth a bit of temper to get a compliment from you," she said with a laugh. "I asked you if you'd been invited to the wedding."

"I'm never invited to weddings," he said good-humouredly.

"Then I should see Sutton and get him to send you a card," she said, and again he saw that malignant smile.

"You're not going, of course?"

"Why 'of course'?" she snapped.

He pushed back his chair from the table, thrust his hands deep in his pockets, his head drooped on one side, an accusative attitude of his, and for a moment she quaked.

"I came into the office rather late last night," he said significantly, and the attack for the moment took her breath away.

"You were here late? What's that to do with me?"

"You were here late, too. And by the peculiar scent of his Egyptian cigarettes, Frank Sutton was in here late."

"Well, why shouldn't he be? And why shouldn't I be?" Her voice was trembling with anger. "I'm his secretary, aren't I? Is there anything wrong with that?"

He did not answer this.

"How long have you known Frank Sutton? Years and years, haven't you? You must have been a very pretty girl when you first came into his employ."

She was on her feet now, white and shaking.

"What the hell do you mean?" she breathed.

But if she thought to storm him into embarrassment, she was mistaken.

"I mean," he said slowly, "you are here with him two nights a week, and there doesn't seem to be any reason for that. I know pretty well the business that goes on in this office, and it isn't vitally necessary for an engaged man to meet his secretary secretly at the office—"

"I suppose you think they ought to meet secretly in a restaurant, don't you?" Her voice was shaking with fury. "Or in the park, when a girl's engaged to another man—sneaking behind his back and trying to get her away from him. Is that your idea?"

But he was unmoved.

"I'm not talking about me, I'm talking about you," he said. "And I'm talking to you for your good. I happen to know something about Frank Sutton's private life. If you imagine that you're the only girl that he meets after hours in his office, you've got a jolt coming."

He thought she was going to fly at him. Her face was no longer beautiful: it was so distorted with fury that he would not have recognized her.

"You liar! You liar!" she screamed. "There's nobody else—I mean, he doesn't see anybody—you paltry thief!... Took you out of the gutter, out of a prison cell, and gave you an honest job—you thief!"

She stopped, gasping for breath, and he accepted the interval of silence.

"I'll tell you something—maybe it will interest you. Frank Sutton is marrying, or thinks he's marrying, a good woman. He may be all people say he is, as white as he looks. But if he isn't, and any harm comes to Beryl Stedman, you look round for a new lover, my friend, for I'll have his life even if I have to break into the condemned cell to get him!"

It was at that moment, when she could only stare at him speechless, her face working, her hands trembling, that Frank Sutton came in. He gave one glance from the man to the girl, and seemed to divine what was happening.

"Hullo, hullo!" he said sharply, and he was addressing the woman. "What's the trouble here? In one of your tantrums, eh? What is it, Leslie?"

John Leslie shrugged his shoulders.

"Miss Trent is a little difficult," he said, rather unjustly.

She tried to speak again, and then, without a word, flew out of the room, slamming the door behind her.

"My dear chap"—Frank's voice was pained, but there was a glint of amusement in his eyes—"why do you quarrel with my Millie?"

Leslie's lips twitched.

"Your Millie! I suggested as much, and that was the cause! In fact, I told her she ought not to be at the office late at night with you, if she valued her good name."

Frank burst into a fit of uncontrollable laughter.

"You never did?" he said, almost admiringly. "Good Lord, I envy you your courage!"

"And then I told her something which may not be true, but she provoked me, and I wished to tantalize her," said Captain Leslie, but did not explain what the provocation was.

"For heaven's sake, leave her alone!" said Frank, the smile still hovering on his face. "She's a perfect devil when she's roused. Poor old Millie! And how stupid you are, Leslie! Of course she's here—not only last night, but dozens of nights! I'm going to enlarge my business after my marriage, and that isn't done without a lot of very private organization. When the scheme is shipshape, you shall see it. Poor old Millie!" he said again, and shook his head, but there was a broad grin on his face when he went out.

Usually, when John Leslie had finished his work, he turned to the newspaper that he brought in with him every morning and made a careful study of certain features. He found this occupation particularly sedative after the little storm of the morning. The agony column revealed nothing profitable, but on the home news page he found two items of supreme interest.

There were in London at that time four international gangs of jewel robbers, who had been operating collectively in places as far removed as Aberdeen is from Plymouth. In reality, as he knew, there were only three of any account: the Dutch gang, which had been responsible for the latest sensation, and two mixed American and English confederations, which had cleaned up well and frequently. It was the latest exploit of one of these—he guessed the Dutch were either out of the country or anxious to leave—that caught his eye. There had been a Park Lane cat burglary, and an Â£8,000 necklace, the property of the Dowager Lady Creethorne, had been lifted while the family were at dinner. It was, said the newspaper report, a very old-fashioned piece of jewellery, set about eighty years before, but the diamonds were good.

The second item was a two-line paragraph, notifying the world that Inspector Barrabal was making a slow recovery.

The cat burglary was two days old, and had been kept quiet at the request of the police. There was published a photograph of the necklace and a long description of each big stone, but this he did no more than skim through.

He had folded away the paper and was standing in the window, staring down into the street as he had stared the night Larry Graeme met his death, when Millie Trent returned. Nobody looking at her would have identified the termagant who had left the room less than half an hour before. She greeted John Leslie with an apologetic smile.

"I'm afraid I rather lost my temper, Captain Leslie," she said, "and I do hope you will forgive me. I'm not feeling my brightest this morning, and anything makes me jumpy. You were trying!"

"I'm afraid I was," said Leslie with a smile.

"No woman likes to have aspersions and innuendoes cast upon her character." She spoke very quickly, and was evidently normal again, for volubility was a characteristic of her more good-natured moments. "I apologize for everything I said about Miss Stedman. She's coming up to the office in a few minutes, and I shouldn't like you to tell her—"

"Coming up to the office?" he said incredulously. "Are you sure?"

She nodded. He did not catch her quick, fleeting smile.

"She's in town, and Mr. Sutton asked her if she'd come up—she and Mr. Friedman."

That was the last news in the world Leslie expected. If he had promised not to approach the girl, the least he expected was that she would be most religiously kept away from the building.

"What time did you come in last night, Captain Leslie? We didn't leave till after half-past eleven."

"About a quarter to twelve," he said; "five minutes after you'd gone."

"What on earth made you come to the office?" she asked with gentle malice. "Surely you're not carrying on a love affair?—Don't be offended."

"I'm not," said Leslie coldly. "I came on my way from the theatre to take away some work. Why do you want to know?"

"I only asked," said Miss Trent.

Sutton's bell summoned her after this, and she went out and was gone a few minutes. When she returned, she was accompanied by a tall, thinnish man with a heavy black moustache, who had "policeman" written all over him, from his square-toed boots to his neatly plastered hair.

"This gentleman wants to see you," she said, and then Frank Sutton came in.

"I say, old man," he said, in a tone of deep concern, "this fellow's got an extraordinary story—this officer, I mean, Sergeant Valentin from Marylebone."

"Sergeant Valentin, C.I.D.," corrected the tall man firmly. "I want to ask you a few questions if you don't mind, Captain Leslie." He looked round. "I don't know that this young lady need stay."

"She had better," said Sutton, "if what you told me is correct."

"True, true," murmured the officer.

He was rather profound, rather tremendous; embodied in his person for the moment all that was awful in the majesty of the law.

"I've had a certain complaint, Captain Leslie—by the way, I happen to know something about your earlier— career."

"Naturally, being a detective sergeant, you know everything," said John Leslie coolly.

"I am inquiring into a robbery that was committed at 804, Park Lane, when the Dowager Lady Creethorne's diamond necklace was stolen. My information is that that necklace is in your possession."

Leslie looked at him steadily.

"Indeed," he said.

"I don't mind telling you that the man who stole the necklace was arrested this morning—at least, one of the men. He said that he parted with the necklace last night at eleven o'clock to a man they all call The Squealer."

"Captain Leslie was here at a quarter to twelve." It was Millie Trent who supplied this information, and the unfeigned satisfaction in her tone she did not attempt to disguise.

"At a quarter to twelve? Well, that would give you plenty of time. The necklace was exchanged on the Thames Embankment at eleven o'clock. The receiver paid the man nine hundred pounds for it in American bills; the same is now in the possession of the police. My information is that you were the receiver."

"Your information is a little cockeyed," said Leslie. "Do you want to search me?"

The police officer looked at him thoughtfully

"You came in here at a quarter to twelve." He took a glance round the room. "Who's got the key of that safe?"

"I have the key of the safe."

"Anybody else got a key?"

"Nobody," said Millie Trent promptly.

"Oh, rubbish!" broke in Sutton. "I have a key somewhere. I never use it, but—"

"You actually have the key in your possession, Mr. Leslie?"

"Captain Leslie," corrected the other. "Yes, it's here."

He took out his key chain and wrenched off a long key from the ring. The detective took it from his hand, turned it in the lock, and drew open the two steel leaves of the safe.

At the back were three steel shelves, empty except for a few account books and

Wrapped in silver tissue paper, some object which he drew out to the light. Frank Sutton uttered an exclamation of amazement as the paper was unfolded; for, on the police sergeant's palm, the dowager's diamond necklace winked dazzlingly in the sunlight.

Frank darted for the door and pulled it open.

"Lew!" he called huskily, and Lew Friedman and the girl came into the room. "Lew, there's an awful mistake here. They've accused Leslie of being—The Squealer! Of having in his possession this." He pointed to the glittering thing in the sergeant's hand.

"Have you come from Scotland Yard?"

It was Leslie's steady voice. He alone was serene: he might have been taking a dispassionate interest in some other man's misfortune.

"Never mind where I'm from"—the sergeant was on his dignity. "I'll trouble you to take a walk with me to Marlborough Street."

"What's the matter with a cab?" asked Leslie. "I hate walking!"

White as death, Beryl Stedman looked at the man who stood stiffly by the table, and, turning his head, John Leslie met her eyes, smiled and shook his head.

"I am The Squealer," he said lightly. "Isn't that an astounding piece of news?"

She did not answer, did not even hear the last word of his sentence; scarcely remembered the trend of it. Suddenly, her knees gave beneath her, and Lew had just time to put his arm about her waist before she fainted.

CHAPTER XVI

BERYL had a very confused recollection of her journey home. Lew told her that she had recovered almost immediately he had taken her down to the car. But she was sitting in a deep armchair in the library at Wimbledon, with the cold air coming gustily through the open casement window, when she became conscious of her own entity.

She awoke, amazingly enough, to find herself in the middle of a vehement argument.

"...not to-day, not to-day," she was saying.

"My dear!" Lew's voice sounded far away, but she knew he was terribly agitated and hurt, and realized that she was the cause. "Frank thinks it best... in view of everything. I want to get you away out of this... Frank has fixed everything... registrar, two o'clock—"

Here he had paused.

"Darling, take an interest." He was shaking her gently. She found herself holding in her trembling hands a long, violet-coloured case. The only thing she was certain about was that it was violet; gold lines were tooled upon it, and there was a beautiful little lock. She opened it without thinking, looked at the pearls, and heard Lew Friedman telling her that it was her wedding present, without fully comprehending the meaning of the phrase.

"I fixed it this morning."

Now she was beginning to understand.

"You fixed it this morning—before—before John's arrest?"

"Yes, I'm glad. It couldn't have happened better."

"But not to-day!" she said wildly. "You don't mean to-day, Lew? You told me that it was to be on Saturday."

"To-day—I think it would be better," he said.

He was dogged; like a man determined to be through with a disagreeable task. For a second, she was resentful, and then she braced herself to face realities. John Leslie was in prison—he was The Squealer—a receiver of stolen property, a traitor to his kind, a betrayer of men who had placed their confidence in him. It was a nauseating thought. She put out her hand, and Lew assisted her to rise, for her legs were still shaky beneath her.

"All right," she breathed. "Any time—when you wish. To-day—any day."

They brought her food, but she could not eat. Lew himself superintended the opening of a bottle of champagne, but she took no more than a sip. When Frank, looking drawn and anxious, came for her, she was her steady self, though still shaken.

"Where is it to be?" she asked.

She did not even marvel at her own calmness. Marriage was like death—a tremendous commonplace that must be faced and endured.

He told her that he had arranged for the marriage to take place at the Wimbledon registrar's office, and it seemed to her that she had heard this before in a dream—that very bad dream from which she had awakened to find herself protesting.

They drove together in Mr. Friedman's Rolls, and ten minutes later she found herself facing a railed desk, behind which sat a bearded man. Somebody said something about witnesses.

"Bring in the chauffeur," said Lew impatiently. "Wait!"

He ran out of the room. The car was nowhere in sight: a policeman had objected to its standing before the door and it had drawn down a side street. But somebody was there whom he dimly remembered having seen before—a dark-faced man with a little black moustache.

"Eh?" he asked. "You're Tillman, aren't you?"

Tillman showed his white teeth in a smile.

"That is my name."

"Come on, you'll do." Lew grasped him by the arm. "We want a witness for my—my niece's marriage. Have you any objection?"

"None whatever," said Tillman cheerfully.

Even in this, her least observant mood, and when certain of her senses were tense, so that the less important occurrences became grotesquely aggrandized, it struck the girl that her future husband was not too pleased to see his clerk, and she remembered that he had not a very high view of Tillman's integrity.

"Hurry," said Lew impatiently, and glanced uneasily at the door.

She had a feeling that, even at this eleventh hour, Lew Friedman expected to see John Leslie stalk into the room and forbid the marriage, and the very thought filled her with hysterical laughter.

It was all over so soon. Almost before the ceremony seemed to have begun, it was ended, and she was signing the register with a shaking hand. And she was Mrs. Frank Sutton; tied for life to the good-natured fellow who was patting her arm encouragingly. She shook hands with Mr. Tillman; he had a large, hearty grip—a powerful-handed man this. She could imagine that he might be the kind who could handle men roughly.

"I won't congratulate you, Mrs. Sutton," he said, "and I will defer my congratulations to your husband for a more appropriate moment."

Mrs. Sutton?

The name was like a blow in the face. And yet there was no reason why it should be. She was married to a good man—the man she loved was a despicable criminal and behind a locked cell door.... She closed her eyes to shut out the picture, and, opening them again, could not see for tears.

No bride had ever left the drab purlieus of a registrar's office with a heart that ached as hers was aching. All the colour and sweetness of life had gone out and left the world a drear desert of a place.

"... Do you think you'll like Scotland?" Frank Sutton was talking, eagerly, nervously.

"I shall love it."

It seemed to Beryl Sutton that it was another woman who answered him.

CHAPTER XVII

THE Squealer was caught. An evening news sheet announced as much—but cautiously.

A man has been detained at Marlborough Street Police Station in connection with the robbery at 804, Park Lane, was the laconic announcement. Only that and no more.

Mr. Joshua Collie did not exactly sit on the steps of Marlborough Street police station—such an act would have been regarded by an outraged constabulary as reprehensible even in one who was so universally a favourite with the police as Joshua Collie. But he did haunt Marlborough Street like an unquiet spirit, buttoning and unbuttoning his overcoat—a trick of his in moments of agitation—and invariably replacing one side of his coat a few inches higher than it was before. Providentially he was near to the entrance of the station when Elford got out of a cab.

"Hullo Joshua!" said the inspector cheerily. "I was talking to Barrabal about you this morning—or rather, he was talking to me. He has a very high opinion of you, and I shouldn't be surprised if you got in on this story before your hateful contemporaries!"

"Who is this fellow, Elford?" Collie jerked his head toward the yawning doors of the station. "Leslie?"

"Didn't you know that? Sutton's manager. We caught him with the goods, my boy."

He was cheerful, as he was undoubtedly entitled to be.

"Is he The Squealer?"

"I shouldn't be surprised," said Elford, "but I'll tell you more about it this evening."

Joshua hung about, and in half an hour Elford came out alone and went whistling toward Regent Street, swinging his gold-headed umbrella and evincing all those kinds of happiness and cheer that police officers display when they have put somebody into a cell with the certainty that they will "go down" for at least ten years.

"Is Barrabal coming?" asked Joshua, overtaking him.

"He has been here," was the reply. "He was here an hour ago and cross-examined Leslie very thoroughly."

He stopped suddenly and faced the little man.

I'm going to give you the story of your life, Collie," he said. "Do you know Miss Beryl Stedman?"

Collie nodded.

"Well, the day she gets married, you stick closer to her than a brother, because I've got an idea you're going to see one of the most interesting murders that has ever been committed!"

"Good gracious!" said Mr. Collie, shocked.

He trotted back to his office with the news of Leslie's arrest, and Field came halfway across the room to meet him.

"Do you know Miss Beryl Stedman?" he asked, unconsciously a plagiarist.

"I know her. Why?"

"She was married this afternoon. Go down to Wimbledon and see if you can get a story."

Mr. Collie took off his straw hat and wiped his brow.

"Married?" he said, in a hollow voice. "How perfectly fascinating!"

His mind for the moment was on interesting murders.

Mr. Tillman had not been invited to the house at Wimbledon. But, nevertheless, he came—which was his way. When Millie Trent arrived in a great hurry by taxicab, she found him sitting in the hall, his hands on his knees, apparently asleep.

"What are you doing here, Tillman?" she asked wrathfully. "Nobody asked you to call."

"Nobody ever invites me anywhere," said Tillman sadly. "That is the worst of being an underling. From your exalted position as confidante to the managing director, I have no doubt I am an incongruous guest at this happy wedding feast."

"I wish to God you wouldn't use such long words!" she snapped.

"I was brought up on long words," said Tillman cheerfully.

She still lingered, a very suspicious woman, and he explained.

"I brought a letter down for the governor. They told me he'd gone to the registrar's office, so I taxied up just in time to be a witness to this romantic marriage. I was invited to the wedding breakfast, so I came."

"Who invited you?" she asked.

"I did," said he calmly. "Nobody else thought of it—it was up to me to remedy the oversight. Mr. Friedman, that excellent Hebrew gentleman, has found me useful. He was in some dilemma as to whether I should eat with the servants or dine at high table, but we compromised with a plate of broken meats in the billiard room."

His flippancy appalled her.

"I've never heard you talk like that before."

"You've missed a treat," he said.

"What are you waiting here for?"

"Mr. Friedman. Curiously enough, he is the proprietor of the house, and it is within his province to invite all and sundry to sit in the vestibule of his handsome mansion. And not even the confidential secretary of the managing director may vary his wishes!"

She was never quite sure whether Tillman was laughing at her, and this uncertainty lay at the bottom of her irritation.

"Where is Mr. Sutton?"

"He's not back yet."

She opened her mouth at this.

"Not back?" incredulously.

"He had to go up to town for something. The telephone rang after he left, and I answered it. It was rather a poetical message: perhaps you will pass it on to him?"

This was a new Tillman. At the office he had been difficult but more or less respectful—generally less. But he had at least assumed no airs, and had never before taken to himself this tone of superiority. It had been a gracious whim of hers to admit him to terms of equality; his present attitude of bantering superiority infuriated her. But she was curious about the message. So far as she knew, no message, poetical or otherwise, was likely to come through to Frank Sutton.

"What was it?" she asked frowning.

He took a leather notebook from his pocket and turned the leaves.

"'The *Empress* goes out on to-morrow's tide'" he said dramatically. "Have you ever heard such poetry?"

"The *Empress* goes out on to-morrow's tide." Her brows were knit in thought as she slowly repeated the words. "I'll tell him. Can you tear that sheet out?"

"To oblige you, I will give you the book," he said graciously. She hated him worst when he was flowery.

Soon after she had disappeared, Friedman came downstairs. He had some telegrams addressed, and Mr. Tillman, an obliging man, had expressed his willingness to serve that day in the most menial capacity.

"You can take them and go back to the office, my boy. And here's a fiver—"

Mr. Tillman raised his hand in protest.

"No, thank you. You have given me a very pleasant memory, Mr. Friedman, one that will last all my life, probably; and if you don't mind, I'd rather stay on until these young people are—um—disposed of, if I may use so gruesome a term."

"Very well," said Lew, and asked: "Have you been on the 'phone to the office—is anything more known about Leslie?"

Tillman shook his head.

"Nothing, except that they say in the evening newspapers that Barrabal has the case in hand. But that," he smiled, "I take leave to doubt."

Lew looked at him suspiciously.

135

"Why do you say that?" he asked. "What do you know about Barrabal?"

"Who knows anything about anybody?" was the evasive reply. "But a man in that position, a man who is not frantically keen to be brought into public prominence, is hardly likely to bother his head about Leslie. It is a mere exercise of logical deduction."

And then he got back to the subject from which he had strayed.

"If it isn't inconvenient to you, I should like to stay around, Mr. Friedman. Possibly I may be of some use."

"Very well," said Lew, after giving the matter a moment's thought. "You can come back, but I don't exactly know what to do with you. You can amuse yourself in the billiard room if you wish—do you play?"

Tillman replied without much enthusiasm that he knocked the balls about a bit, and went off on his errand. For a few minutes, Lew Friedman wandered aimlessly from room to room, and then, after standing hesitant at the foot of the stairs, he went slowly up and knocked on the door of Beryl's room. It was a little suite really, sitting room and bedroom being connected by an arched opening.

She was resting on the broad window seat, looking out into the garden, when he came in.

"Well, my dear?"

"Well, my dear?" It was brave of her to mock him when her heart was so heavy and life seemed such a blank and purposeless vista.

He sat down in the window seat by her side and took her hand.

"Everything is going to be quite all right. And I want to tell you something that will please you."

She looked at him listlessly. There were so few things that could please her at that moment.

"I've told my solicitor to engage the biggest man at the Bar to defend our unfortunate friend," he said, and saw the light come into her eyes, and then a film of tears.

"How sporting of you, Lew!" she said in a low voice. "And how like you!" She squeezed his hand between both hers. "It doesn't seem possible, does it, that a man like—John Leslie should be so unutterably—mean! I think that is what has hurt me—not that he"—she hesitated—"is a thief, but he's this—what is the vile word?—Squealer. That is the dreadful part of it: men trusted him and he betrayed them whenever it suited his purpose."

Her thoughtful eyes roved the garden for a while and then came back to him.

"I don't believe it," she said.

He was astonished.

"You don't believe it? But, my dear, he admitted he was The Squealer—you heard him!"

She shook her head.

"No, I remember now—I remember the tone of sarcasm in his voice. It was his way to accept other people's estimates of him. Where is my—husband? That sounds awfully queer, doesn't it?"

"He has had to go to town," Lew hastened to explain. "You see, my dear, this thing was fixed up in such a hurry, and he has so many jobs to do, with Leslie being away. Frank has to appoint somebody to take his place."

It was raining, a fine persistent drizzle from heavy clouds. It would be raining all night... when she was on her way to Scotland... when John Leslie was turning uneasily upon his plank bed. She screwed her eyes tight. With his quick intuition, he knew what she was thinking about.

"Don't let your mind dwell on it," he said. And then, in a tone of raillery: "My dear, do you know what you've cost me to-day? A small fortune! You know how we Jews hate giving money away—you must have read it in the comic papers—we Ikeys and Levys and Cohens."

She put her hand on his knee and patted him.

"Don't be silly, please."

"Forty thousand pounds!" he said dramatically. "And that is apart from your settlement. I gave Frank a check for twenty thousand, and he sent his woman secretary up to the bank with it—a shrewd fellow, Frank. He showed

138

me his scheme for enlarging the business. He ought to be a millionaire before he dies."

He was chatting on when she interrupted him, pointing.

"Who is that?"

From where they sat, they could see over an angle of fence the main road which crosses the common. A woebegone figure in a bedraggled straw hat and a long fawn overcoat was standing, looking up at the house.

"By Jove, I think it's that little reporter from the *Post-Courier*"

"Poor soul, he looks drowned!" she said. "Have him in and give him some tea, Lew. He has only come to inquire about the wedding."

Her voice was eager; he wondered a little at her enthusiasm, and, shrewd as he was, did not suspect that she wanted to talk to the reporter and get from him the latest news of Leslie.

Lew went downstairs and sent a footman to summon the wayfarer to the house. Joshua was wet, but apparently unconcerned. His straw hat, he said, regarding it affectionately, had weathered five winters and was good for another five. Somebody must have valeted him, for every button of his overcoat was in its right place.

"I've nothing to tell you, my boy, except what you probably know, that Mr. Sutton is married. If you want particulars, I dare say Tillman will supply them."

"Tillman!"

It was difficult to know whether Joshua was aghast or just merely interested. The word had a hollow sound.

"Is *he* here? Dear me, how strange! In fact, how remarkable!"

Beryl interrupted the discussion. She took Joshua by the arm, led him, almost dragged him, into a little sitting room opening from the hall, and was so cheerful that Lew Friedman could have fallen on Joshua Collie's neck in gratitude. But with that sense of relief he began to understand the cause for her enthusiasm, and wisely left them alone.

She put her question almost before her guardian was out of hearing.

"No, I have not seen Captain Leslie," said Joshua.

"Mr. Collie"—she was very urgent—"could you *please* do me a favour? Would you go back to town and take some money for him? He may want extra food or something. Perhaps you could see him and tell him that Mr. Friedman is engaging counsel for him? I would rather you didn't—tell him about my being married. There is plenty of time for him to know that. Would you do this for me?"

Joshua scratched his chin thoughtfully.

140

"Naturally, I will do anything I possibly can. They may not allow me to see him, because, as you can imagine, my unfortunate position may prevent that. One of the trials of a newspaper reporter's life is that he is never allowed to interview interesting crim—er—prisoners."

"But it would be possible to send a note to him. Could you return and tell me?" she asked quickly. "Perhaps he has a message to send to me."

She opened her little handbag, took out a bundle of notes, and would have given them all to him.

"One will be sufficient," said Joshua, "and I shall be able to place that in the care of the inspector. I understand that it is possible to obtain little extra luxuries. Mr. Tillman was at your wedding?"

She nodded.

"Yes, he was a witness. Do you know him?"

Joshua's eyes wandered past her.

"I know of him," he said. "You have not spoken to him about Captain Leslie?"

"I?" she answered in surprise. "No. Why? Would it be of any use?"

But in his vague way he passed the question.

"If I were you, Miss Stedman" (she blessed him for the name), he said, lowering his voice to a hoarse, confidential whisper, "I don't think I'd discuss Captain Leslie at all. You might ask him... no, I don't think I'd even ask him. I feel rather horrid in making this suggestion, but I know that you are concerned about the captain, and knowing this I feel that the best interests of all parties would be served if... you understand?"

She nodded.

"Very well, then," said Joshua, in triumph. "Mum's the word!"

CHAPTER XVIII

HE WAS gone before Tillman returned from his errand, and Beryl found a new interest in watching Frank Sutton's clerk. He was obviously a very capable man: not the sort, one would have imagined, who wanted the "chance" that Frank had given him. He had something of the litheness of a tiger, and in his dark, eager face was that questing look that she associated with a certain type of restless vitality.

She had ample opportunity for making an observation, for Frank had not returned from the City, and Lew seemed to have given Tillman the run of the house.

Millie Trent, who had brought down a big attache case full of papers, monopolized the drawing room. Beryl did not like her, and it amused her to watch the antagonism between Frank's secretary and Tillman. Whenever they met, they seemed to snap, although, to do him justice, the explosions were all on Millie's side.

Tillman had taken up his station in the hall, an act which seemed to irritate the woman.

"Can't you find some other place to sit?" Beryl heard her say.

"I'd be sitting in the drawing room if you weren't there," was Tillman's prompt reply.

Another time when she came out, Tillman said:

143

"No call."

"What do you mean, 'no call'?" demanded Millie.

"You're expecting a telephone call, and it hasn't come through," was the cool reply.

"Mind your own business!"

Beryl, through the open door of the library, heard all this and was occupied, and devoutly glad to be occupied, for there were certain matters she did not wish to think about.

There was a telephone instrument at the far end of the hall, and evidently Tillman was right in his surmise, for when the bell shrilled and he rose to answer, the woman flew out of the room and reached the instrument first.

It was a message from Frank Sutton, saying he was on his way.

"Oh, joy!" murmured Tillman provocatively as she passed, and she spun round.

"I don't get you," she said in an ominous tone.

"Nobody gets me," said Tillman. "I'm known as the Prize that Cannot be Won!"

"You're going to lose a good job," she fired at him, and Beryl heard him chuckle.

"Not such a good job as you think," he said. "I am rather tired of adding up columns of meaningless figures about non-existing exports."

Beryl frowned at this, and expected a sharp retort, but none came, except the banging of the drawing-room door.

After three or four minutes, however, Millie's voice sounded again, and her tone was much milder.

"What do you mean about 'non-existing exports'?" she asked.

"All exports are non-existent unless you can see them," said Tillman calmly. "Figures mean nothing to me: I have no imagination, and being a materialist, I must see the actual bales and boxes or, as I say, they do not exist."

"You're a fool!" was the reply.

There was no further diversion until the arrival of Frank Sutton, and at the sound of his car's wheels, Beryl's heart began to thump painfully.

"Hullo, Tillman! What the devil are you doing here?"

"On duty, sir," said Tillman, and Frank laughed.

"I shall be making you manager one of these days."

"God forbid!" said the other piously, and this Sutton regarded as a huge joke, for he was roaring with laughter when he came in to the girl.

"I've had a perfectly poisonous afternoon, my dear." He sat down by her side and his arm went round her shoulder. "You've no idea what a mess we're in at the office. Fortunately, Miss Trent knows most of my business, and she'll be able to keep things straight. To make matters worse, one of my more disreputable clients insisted upon my going to see him at the Leopards—"

"The Leopards?" It was Lew Friedman's amazed voice. "You don't mean the Leopards Club?" he asked as he came in, a half smile on his face.

Frank nodded.

"Good Lord!"

"Do you know it?" asked Frank. Whether he was shocked or surprised, Beryl could not be certain.

"Well—yes," Lew hesitated. "I know the man who runs it—an old soldier named Anerley. I helped him a bit, years ago."

Frank was curious.

"Have you ever been to the club—lately?" he asked.

Apparently Lew was not prepared to answer this question without consideration.

"I met Anerley in Jo'burg after the war—a good fellow in many ways, though he is an awful tough. A few years ago I met him again. He had a chance of buying the Leopards— they had got into some sort of trouble and had been struck off. Bill thought his war service would count in getting it back, and he was right."

But Frank was insistent upon one point.

"Have you been there lately?"

Again the question was evaded.

"Why, it must be twenty years since I first went to the place! It's on the third floor, isn't it? You went up by a lift, and there was a jolly fine fire escape down which you could slide when the police raided you, as they did every other week."

Beryl wanted to keep the conversation on this line, was desperate in her anxiety. She did not wish them to speak of marriage, or her, or this ghastly trip.

"Yes, it can't be a very bright spot," said Lew.

Then it was that he remembered the telegram that had come on the previous night. Possibly he was anxious to turn the conversation into other channels.

"I can't find it," he said, searching the library table, "but it went somehow like this: 'Berth arranged for Jacksons. Pacific.'"

"Berth arranged for what?"

He heard the harsh voice and looked round in surprise, and observed Millie Trent come into the room, and her attitude was, to say the least, a little truculent.

"That's nothing to do with you," said Frank roughly. "I don't want you yet, Miss Trent."

Lew had the impression that she was in an overpowering rage and was utilizing every ounce of will power to get herself under control.

"I'll be in the drawing room if you want me," she said, and walked out.

"Humph!" said Lew. His tone and his manner were alike grave. "Strange woman, that!"

Frank shrugged.

"She's been with me for fourteen years," he said awkwardly. "She's a little difficult at times."

"Yes," said Lew, and his tone was gruff.

When Beryl had gone back to her room:

"Play me a game of billiards, Lew?" said the younger man. "I'm rather on edge."

"That's not a good mood for billiards," said Lew.

He raised his finger, enjoining silence: he was waiting until he heard the door of Beryl's room close, and when the thud of it came down, he asked:

"What is this woman to you?"

"To me?" Frank appeared to be thunderstruck by the question. "You mean Millie Trent?"

"I mean Millie Trent."

"What has she to do....? Why, good heavens, you don't imagine..."

"I'm not imagining anything, I'm just asking you," said Lew harshly. "I'm telling you this, Frank, that if there is any—friendship between you and Miss Trent, it ends to-day! I know men, and I know how even the nicest of them make fools of themselves over impossible women. If that has been the case, and you want money to buy her off, I'll let you have all you need. But I'm telling you that Beryl's happiness is the first, the last, and every consideration to me."

Frank slipped his arm affectionately into the other's.

"My dear Lew," he said, "I'd hate you if it wasn't! It has been a perfectly rotten time for my darling and you. Gosh, I wish I could help that fellow Leslie!"

"That's like you," smiled Lew, as he led the way to the billiard room.

As they were turning out of the hall, Frank saw the sitting Tillman.

"You don't want this chap, do you?"

"He asked to be allowed to stay. He may be very useful."

"I don't know exactly how," laughed Frank, as he selected a cue.

They had been playing for five minutes when Friedman remembered the fuming secretary.

"Let her wait," said the other carelessly. "I've got a lot of beastly papers to go through, and there is tons of time."

Miss Trent was not the sort of person who would possess her soul in patience. Twice she appeared at the billiard-room door with a face as black as thunder, and twice the business interview was postponed. The sounding of the dinner gong brought relief to at least one mind.

CHAPTER XIX

THAT dinner...! Lew never forgot the strain of it. Every line of conversation seemed forced and unnatural. Frank's nerves were obviously on edge, and after a while he infected his host with a like jumpiness.

They were crawling through the dessert and coffee stage when Mr. Joshua Collie was announced. The girl rose from the table quickly.

"I think he wants to see me," she said, and hurried out of the room.

But Lew was taking no risks: she was hardly in the hall before he had followed her. To his surprise, Tillman had disappeared, and the only person in the broad vestibule besides the footman who had admitted him was Joshua Collie, the contours of whose straw hat were painful to see.

"Well, Mr. Collie?" It was Lew who put the question. "What is your news—good or bad?"

He pushed open the door of the library and himself assisted the reporter out of his coat. Beryl saw through the manoeuvre: if there was any message from John Leslie, she was not to receive it, and for a moment she grew hot with anger. And then the helplessness of it all struck her. What did it matter—what did anything matter?

To her surprise, Friedman came straight to the point when he asked bluntly:

"Well, have you got a message from Leslie?"

Joshua coughed.

"No," he said very carefully, "there is no message from Captain Leslie—for anybody."

Lew grunted his satisfaction.

"That is good—" he began.

"There is no message," continued Joshua, "because I could find no person to give the message. In fact, Captain Leslie has been released on bail."

Lew's face was a picture of bewilderment.

"Released on bail?" he said incredulously. "A man who has been a convict and is now charged with a felony... released on bail?"

"I thought it was rather remarkable myself," said Joshua. "In fact, I said to the inspector in charge: 'This is rather extraordinary, isn't it?'"

"He's not in prison?" asked Beryl. "Thank God for that!"

"He's not in prison—not even at Marlborough Street, which is merely a house of temporary detention. He is not in his lodgings, he is not at the office. In fact," he said, with beaming candour, "I don't know where he is,"

Sutton had followed them and had heard the astonishing news, and the effect upon him was remarkable. His face had gone pale, the eyes seemed to have sunk into his head.

"Leslie released?" he asked huskily. "You're mistaken!"

"I'm never mistaken." Joshua's very tone was a reproof. "I know or I don't know. All I know are facts, and it is a fact that Captain Leslie has been released on bail. It is a remarkable occurrence. As I said to the inspector in charge—"

"Yes, yes," said Lew impatiently; "we know what you said to the inspector in charge. But when did this happen?"

"Apparently," said Joshua, "after the visit of Inspector Barrabal. Whether Inspector Barrabal visited him at all," continued the exasperating man, "or whether Mr. Elford, whose unveracity is one of the scandals of Scotland Yard, was pulling my—um"—he looked dubiously at Beryl—" pulling my leg, in a manner of speaking, I am not in a position to state. The only thing I know is that Leslie walked out of Marlborough Street and took a taxicab to an unknown destination."

A deep, almost painful, silence followed this third and definite pronouncement.

"Extraordinary!" said Lew. He spoke with an effort, and braced himself as if to meet some unpleasant consequence. He looked at his watch and nodded. "I don't think it matters very much," he said briskly. "Will you have a drink, Mr. Collie?"

Mr. Collie thought he would like a drink.

"Go into the drawing room; I'll send Tillman in to you."

"I think I ought to say," said Collie, as he was halfway across the hall, "that the inspector in charge at Marlborough Street said that never in all his experience..."

"I'm sure," said the impatient Mr. Friedman, and almost pushed the reporter into the presence of one who, expecting somebody else, found it difficult to compose her face.

"Hullo, what do you want?" she asked ungraciously.

"Refreshment," said Joshua, and rubbed his hands expectantly.

There were a tantalus, a syphon, and glasses. Evidently Miss Trent had found her way to this without assistance, for one of the glasses had been used.

'What do you want here?" she asked.

"I am what is known as a Mercury," he beamed. "In other words, I am a bearer of tidings, both glad and bad."

She was all attention now.

"What is the bad?" she asked.

Mr. Collie was unusually loquacious. What, he said, was one man's meat was another man's poison. One man's good news struck terror to another.

"For God's sake, don't gas so much," said the woman. "What has happened?"

He looked at her meditatively.

"Captain John Leslie has been released on bail."

She wilted under the shock, stepped back as though he had struck her.

"I don't believe it," she said, and the arrival of the reluctant Tillman put an end to her further questions.

"Get Mr. Collie a drink," she said, and went swiftly from the room.

Tillman evidently had found his way to the tantalus before, but before he did anything further, he closed the door which Millie had left open.

"Well, what are you doing here?" he asked. His voice was stern, almost commanding. "You're wasting your time at Wimbledon."

Joshua smiled sheepishly.

"In a sense I am doing the same as you," he said. "I also am conducting a little private investigation in my own tin-pot way. I do that sort of thing for a living. And if Wimbledon is good enough for you, it is a desirable hunting ground for me. You may not know—"

"Oh, I know all right," interrupted Tillman. He poured out the whisky. "Say 'when.'"

"I don't know the word," said Collie. "Use your discretion."

And then, as Tillman splashed in the soda water:

"I recognized you the moment I saw you—once I've seen a man I never forget him."

154

He took the glass from Tillman's hand, raised it critically to the light.

"Here's luck to the happy bride!" he said. "If she is happy."

Tillman was regarding him with an unfavourable eye.

"I wondered if you knew me. I had an idea we'd met somewhere."

"At the Corthurst murder trial—I saw you in court," murmured Joshua. "Chelmsford, three years ago—or was it four?... They keep a very good beer at the Red Lion. Have you ever been to Hereford? I was there for a murder trial some years ago. You know the place I mean? The Mitre is an excellent hotel. They have rather a good cellar of port."

"I was wondering if you remembered me and hoping you didn't," said Tillman.

He poured out a small portion of whisky, put in a liberal allowance of soda water and sipped it daintily.

"You hadn't got a moustache in those days," reflected Collie, "but I never forget a man's walk—you know my methods, Watson.

"Eh?" said Tillman, doubting his ears. "My name may not be Tillman, but it certainly isn't Watson."

"Then you don't know my methods," said Collie calmly. "That's unfortunate."

Tillman took the glass from his hand.

"Have another drink—it isn't mine."

"Very sorry," murmured Mr. Collie. "Somebody was rather curious to-night—wanted to know if I'd ever seen you before. Let me see, who was it?... Yes, the Trent girl. You're getting the sack: I suppose you know that?"

They laughed together.

"I'll be glad to get it," said Tillman drily.

Joshua looked round and came closer to his companion.

"You wouldn't like to tell me what you've discovered? I see by your pained expression that you wouldn't." There was a pause. "Perhaps," he said, "I can give you a little news— Captain John Leslie has been released."

He said this a little dramatically, and the effect was disappointing. Tillman's faint smile was very knowledgeable.

"So I believe," he said. "I should have been very surprised if he wasn't."

He heard a noise in the hall, opened the door, and looked out.

"The trousseau is leaving," he said, and stepped aside to allow Beryl to come in.

She went straight across to Joshua.

"Mr. Collie," she said in a low voice, "if I addressed a letter to you at the *Post-Courier* you would get it, wouldn't you?"

Joshua smiled sadly.

"Yes. Mark it 'Private' and then it'll only be opened twice."

She would have said more, but Lew Friedman, who shadowed her when she was talking to the reporter, was already in the room.

"Well, Mr. Collie"—he was geniality itself—"I don't know that we can give you any further news. I've nothing sensational for you."

Joshua was pained.

"I wouldn't take it if you had," he said. "We make our own sensations." He looked slyly at Lew. "We haven't had one in the paper for ten years—the night the police raided the Leopards Club and several middle-aged gentlemen had to get away by the fire escape!"

Lew's face was a study, and then he laughed.

"Gosh! you've got a very good memory for faces! Were you with the police?"

Joshua shook his head.

"No, I was a little ahead of the police. I got away before they recognized me—I remember passing you on the fire escape!"

Lew shook his head.

"They were mad days, eh? Leopards Club? Funny thing, I was only talking to my—to Mr. Sutton about the club to-night. He's a member still; he tells me it's going strong."

157

Beryl had gone; Tillman, in some mysterious fashion, had sidled from the room, and they were alone.

"Yes, it is still going strong," said Mr. Collie. "They've had a new fire escape put in—you can get away four abreast."

They went out into the hall to find Frank Sutton waiting. Somewhere in the background hovered the grim figure of Millie Trent. Sutton frowned at the reporter.

"You're not giving the press any information, are you, Lew?" he asked quickly. "I mean, about the marriage?" And to Collie: "What are you writing about this wedding?"

"Nothing," said Joshua. "You might get a paragraph in the *Wimbledon Gazette*, but the great heart of London, E.C.4 will not be stirred by the happy intelligence—except at our advertisement rate. Wimbledon marriages," he reflected, "are not news—they are inevitable, like the annual rainfall."

There was a dramatic interruption to Joshua Collie's views. A footman appeared in the doorway.

"Well?" asked Friedman.

"Somebody wishes to see you, sir—Captain Leslie!"

There was a dead silence. Collie's eyes were fixed upon Sutton; he saw him change colour.

"Show him in," said Lew Friedman's harsh voice.

CHAPTER XX

"WHAT—" began Frank, but the other silenced him with a gesture.

"Show him in. You had better go, Collie."

Mr. Collie went without protest.

There was another long silence, and then John Leslie entered slowly; looked from one man to the other.

"Well?" said Mr. Friedman.

"I want to see Sutton." Leslie's voice was hard, menacing.

"Well, you're seeing him," said Friedman loudly. "I admitted you, Leslie, because I trust you. But there's going to be no rough-house. If there is, I'm in it."

"What a good fellow you are, Friedman! I think I've told you before, I've a hell of a good opinion of Jews since I met you."

Friedman nodded curtly.

"That's all right—but no rough-house. You're a lucky man to be free to-night. The law has changed a bit, hasn't it?"

Leslie was looking fixedly at Sutton.

"It's just about the same—penal servitude for receivers and trouble for squealers."

Friedman was alert, watchful; his one object was to avoid trouble.

"I thought the police liked a squealer," he said good-humouredly.

Leslie nodded.

"Yes, for a time. They use him and use him and use him; then one day they say: 'We've got all we can out of this fellow—go and pull him in.' That is, when you know him."

"Now, listen to me, Leslie," said Lew. "I want to do something for you. Is a thousand any good to you?"

For the first time Sutton spoke.

"I bear you no malice, Leslie—" he began, but the manager interrupted him.

"You've used it all up, haven't you?"

He turned slowly to Friedman.

"I'll do you a turn. If you've any spare thousands, pass them over to Sutton! Let him get out of this country quick. There's a boat leaving for Canada to-morrow morning—there's time to catch the train."

Lew Friedman sighed heavily.

"Oh, you're not going to be sensible, eh?"

Leslie's finger went up and pointed to the white-faced Sutton.

"You know what you're getting for a son-in-law, don't you? You're getting The Squealer—the biggest fence in London!"

Friedman smiled and shook his head.

"A skunk that's put more poor devils in prison than any police officer. You'll be lucky if you get away with a whole skin."

"Did he make you a convict?" asked Friedman.

"I made myself a convict," replied the other roughly. "I take all the credit."

"Now, look here, Leslie." Again Lew Friedman tried to stem the gathering storm. "I don't want to quarrel with you. You're sore with Sutton over another matter. We won't mention names. I know how you feel; I can sympathize with you. But I've got somebody's happiness to consider."

"So have I," said Leslie quickly. "Sutton, if you marry Beryl Stedman, look out—by God, I'll kill you!"

He moved toward Frank, but Friedman came between them.

"You're a lunatic!" he swore. "There's no sense in you! Suppose you do a little bit of looking out too, eh? Up to a point, I'm an easy man, but you're going beyond it, Leslie. I've got something to say in this, haven't I?"

For the first time he was seeing John Leslie in a cold fury. The man's face was white and tense.

"Let Sutton speak—hasn't he got a tongue? Have you got to nurse him all the time?" he demanded angrily.

Sutton laughed, and there was something unnatural in his laugh.

"Don't you worry about me: I can take care of myself!"

"Can you?" said the other sardonically. "You've been looking after yourself since you started that fake business of yours. You were looking after yourself when you put me in all ready for sacrifice, as you put in your earlier managers."

"You're a damned liar!" snarled Sutton.

Lew Friedman shook his head helplessly.

"Get it off your chest and go, will you, Leslie?"

"A fake business with faked books!" Leslie accused. "All your real work is done in your little car or at the Leopards Club."

He saw Friedman start.

"That's where you met the fly men and bought their sparklers—I'm warning you, Sutton."

Lew heard a sound upstairs, walked to the door quickly, and opened it. Then he turned.

"That's the finish," he said. "Clear!"

But Leslie had not finished.

"Cut out that marriage scheme, Sutton! Stick to your old graft."

And then Friedman's hand fell on his shoulder, and his voice was urgent.

"Get out through the garden, Leslie—oblige me. There's a tradesman's gate round the corner of the house."

John paused irresolutely.

"I'm asking you as a favour."

"All right," nodded the other. "Miss Stedman's coming, I suppose?"

He walked to the long French windows, pulled one open, and paused.

"You don't know what I'm doing for you, Sutton," he said, and in a second he had vanished into the dark.

Sutton was breathing heavily, but, as he took a step toward the window, Friedman put out his hand and drew him back.

"That'll do," he growled. "The time to get fierce was when he was here. Put a grin on, will you?"

"Did you hear him—what he said?" breathed Frank Sutton. "Accused me! My God, what a colossal nerve the fellow has—"

Lew pinched his arm till he winced. Beryl had come in. They watched her as she carried her attaché case to the writing table and sat down. She pulled open the drawer, evidently searching for old documents to destroy. She was dressed ready for the journey, and there was that in her face which made the Jew's heart ache. Never had he seen tragedy so clearly written.

"Can I help you, honey?" he asked, a little huskily.

She shook her head.

"No, I'd rather do this alone, if you don't mind."

She hadn't heard Leslie's voice, then. Lew breathed a deep sigh. At least she had been spared that shock.

163

"You've a whole lot of time, Beryl," he said. "You needn't leave the house for another two hours."

She nodded at this, took a sheet of note-paper, and waited. The gesture of dismissal was not lost upon Sutton.

"Can't you leave that, Beryl?" he asked, and something of his inward agitation was reflected in his voice. He was irritable, impatient: but, try as he did, he could not wholly recover his old suave tone.

"Come along." It was Lew who took him by the arm. "Let's go along and throw Tillman out and have the house to ourselves, without clerks and reporters."

"I think Beryl ought to know—" began Sutton.

He had lost his nerve; required the support which her knowledge of Leslie's threat would give him.

"Shut up!" whispered Lew fiercely. "What are you talking about, you fool?"

Before Frank Sutton could speak, he was hustled out of the room and the door closed, leaving the girl alone.

She gazed after them, an expression of wonder on her face. What ought she to know? Then, with a shrug of despair, she dipped her pen in the ink. This was the sixth attempt to write, and it must be successful. In her heart was a sense of thankfulness that the man she loved was at least at liberty. That was the thought she was carrying away with her.

She wrote a few lines, stopped to read them, had an overwhelming desire to tear up the page, but successfully resisted the temptation. She had written a word when the sound of the French windows opening brought up her head in alarm.

For a second, she could not believe her eyes, and then, with a little cry, she rose, and in another instant was sobbing in John Leslie's arms. He held the quivering figure tight, whispering incoherent words into her ear.

"Oh, my dear, my dear!" she sobbed. "They let you go?"

He looked at the door: no sound came from the hall outside.

"Yes. They were not quite sure that I was the culprit."

"I've been so worried, so unhappy. I was just writing you a letter. I was sending it to Mr. Collie to give to you."

His eyes were still on the door.

"Is anybody likely to come in?" he asked.

She shook her head.

"No. They've gone to the billiard room."

Gently she disengaged herself, went to the door and, opening it, listened. There came to her ears the click of billiard balls. She closed the door firmly. There was the tiniest little bolt, and, after a moment's hesitation, she shot this.

"Miss Trent is here, but she's in the library. Oh, John, you don't know how happy you've made me!"

He held her at arm's length.

"To see me?"

She nodded.

"To see you—free." And then, with a pathetic little smile: "You're such a dreadful character! How could you, John! I'm so hurt about it."

He was holding her by the shoulders, looking hungrily into her eyes.

"A man like myself has to be many things," he said. "Beryl, I've got something to say to you.

She knew what that something was, tried to free herself, but he held her shoulders firmly.

"No, no, please! Don't say it."

"I shall have to... I've said it once. You see, I—well, I love you! I can't lose you without a fight, can I?"

"Don't!" she murmured in a low voice.

"I must," he said. "I should be mad if I didn't tell you. Beryl, whatever you do, whomever you marry, you can't marry this man."

He read the despair in her face, and his heart stood still. Before she spoke the words, he knew.

"I'm married," she whispered, and he dropped his hands.

CHAPTER XXI

"MARRIED?" he asked, in horror. "You're joking!"

She shook her head.

"Married—when?"

She told him.

"We had a special licence. It wasn't to be until—to-morrow, but Lew wished to have it over, because—well, because of what happened this morning, John. He knows... how I feel about you."

Married! There was murder in his eyes as he moved toward the door, but she clung to his arm.

"Don't, don't! What are you going to do?"

"I'm going to settle with Frank Sutton," he said between his teeth.

"You mustn't! Jack, you won't?"

She clung to him desperately, her arms about his neck.

"For God's sake, don't! It's no worse for you than it is for me—haven't you any instinct? Can't you see what it means to me? I'm only just awake... I thought knowing you and all those meetings were just pleasant little interludes, and now I know—I know."

She was weeping softly on his breast, and all the fury died out of his heart. He had wanted to save her this, he told her—he was a brute. Suddenly, her weeping ceased, and she put him away from her.

"I love you, that's the truth," she said in a low voice. "It's no use being a fool and pretending I don't. It would kill Uncle Lew—if I—did what I want to do. But I've got to go through with it now, John, haven't I? I've got to go through with it?"

He shook his head slowly.

"My dear, don't lose hold of yourself. We've all—got to go through with it. When do you leave?"

She was dabbing her eyes with a little handkerchief.

"Ten-something from King's Cross," she said listlessly. "Jack, you're not going to do anything or say anything— you're not?"

"Ten-something," he nodded.

"You're not going to do anything that will hurt you and me, are you? Jack, are you? Why don't you answer me?"

He spoke half in thought.

"Married you—the cur! God! I'd have spared him something if he hadn't done that!"

He was frightening her. And then she heard quick footsteps coming down the stairs.

"Go into the garden: there's somebody coming—please, please!"

She put up her face and kissed him, and, as he disappeared through the French windows, she flew to the door, drew the bolt noiselessly, and made her way back to the writing table. She was hardly seated when Millie Trent came in. She was carrying a large portfolio, and was evidently on the point of leaving the house, for her hat was on and she wore a long rainproof coat. She was startled at the sight of Beryl.

"Hullo! I didn't know you were here, Miss—Mrs. Sutton. You gave me a fright," she said, a little awkwardly.

"Did you wish to see Mr. Sutton?"

Millie nodded, and the girl had the feeling that for some reason she could not trust her voice.

"I've been trying to speak to him all the afternoon."

Her voice was shrill and strange; had Beryl a knowledge of the woman, she would have known that Millie Trent was half mad with anger.

"Whenever I try to speak to him, he goes to the billiard room." And then, desperately: "I wish you would ask him to see me, Miss—Mrs. Sutton."

Beryl got up from her chair.

"Yes, I'll call him with pleasure."

"Thank you very much." A pause. "I suppose I ought to call you 'madam'?"

Beryl's lips curled.

"I suppose so—madam!"

The woman heard her call Frank by name at the door of the billiard room, and, setting her portfolio on the desk, she took the seat that Beryl had vacated and glanced with a sour smile at the three lines of writing she read.

Evidently this last summons was to be obeyed. Frank Sutton came quickly into the room and shut the door.

"Have you seen this?" She held up the letter.

He took it from her hand and read:

My   dear   Jack:
I shall not see you again, but I want to tell you that I shall never forget

"'Dear Jack'? Leslie, I suppose."

"She'll see him again all right," said Millie grimly.

The atmosphere was charged with electricity: he felt it, and grew more nervous.

"Where is the money?" he asked.

She opened the portfolio and took out three wads of American currency.

"A hundred and two thousand dollars," she said. "There was nearly a hitch about cashing Friedman's check—I only got to the bank a quarter of an hour before it closed."

"I suppose you sent the other money on to Rome?"
She nodded.

"A pity you couldn't sell the business."

"A great pity," he said.

Their conversation was the spluttering of a fuse. The explosion was to come.

"Where does the car pick me up?" she asked. She was not looking at him, and was playing with a paper knife on the table.

"Eh? Oh, the car? Yes, that picks you up at the corner of Lower Regent Street. You'll just make the Havre boat."

"I'll just make the Havre boat?" she repeated. "Aren't you coming?"

"I'll pick you up at Southampton. You'll want some of this." His fingers ran rapidly over the note pad; he pulled out a few and dropped them in front of her, and she put them in her bag.

"You're coming on after, aren't you?" And then, very deliberately: "The *Empress* goes out on the tide!"

He started.

"I don't know what you mean."

"The *Empress* goes out on the tide—you treacherous dog!"

Her eyes were blazing with rage. "Listen, Mr. Squealer. I've stood a whole lot from you. I've stood imprisonment for you. I've helped you with your dirty graft, and I've stood by and watched you marry five different girls—but you've always left them at the church door."

He licked his dry lips, but made no reply.

"I've been with you in this graft, fencing and squealing. Every squeal you've put in to the police I've typewritten for you! I've carried your diamonds to Antwerp and Paris and risked a life sentence for you!"

"I don't know what you're getting at." His voice was trembling. "What's the matter with you, Millie?"

They did not see the figure that had emerged from the gloom and was standing in the shadow of the window. John Leslie, his head bent, listened, a grim smile on his face.

"I'll tell you what I mean." Millie's voice was a hiss of sound. "You're sending me to Southampton. Do you think I'll fall for that kind of trick? And where are you going? Not to Scotland with this girl—you're taking her to Canada! You've booked the passage in the name of Jackson. The boat train leaves Euston to-night almost at the same time as the train leaves King's Cross for Scotland. I've stood for your bigamy when you left them flat at the church, with their fathers' checks in your pocket, but I'm not standing this!"

"Hush!" he warned her frantically. "Keep your voice down, you damned fool! Somebody will hear you."

"They'll hear soon enough. You're not leaving for Canada and you're not leaving for Scotland—get that, Mr. Squealer! I'm your wife, your only legal wife, and you're coming away with me to Southampton, or I'm going to find Tillman."

"Tillman?"

"Ah!" She laughed harshly. "You don't know who Tillman is, but I can guess."

He was trembling like a leaf, his face the colour of chalk.

"You're mad, Millie!" he gasped. "You wouldn't do a dirty trick like that on me...."

"Are you coming with me?"

He was a quick thinker, The Squealer, and now his brain was racing to find a solution.

"The train doesn't leave till after ten," he said urgently. "Let's talk this over. We can't talk here. Meet me at the Leopards Club in an hour's time."

He saw the suspicion in her eyes and grew almost frenzied in his appeal.

"You fool, if I don't turn up, you can be at the station, can't you? You've nearly two hours to catch me if I don't keep my promise."

"I tell you—" she began.

Suddenly he clapped his hand in front of her mouth.

"They'll hear you in the hall," he whispered.

The door into the hall was ajar, and he almost ran across the room to close it. When he came back, he saw by her face that he had triumphed.

"At the Leopards Club in an hour. I swear to you, Millie, that you're misjudging me. I've no more intention of—"

"You're a liar," she said more calmly, "but I'll take a chance. If you're not there in sixty minutes, I'll be waiting on the platform at Euston, with two 'busies' to pinch you, and enough evidence to send you to Dartmoor for as long as you live. And everybody shall know—John Leslie and Lew Friedman—"

"Hush, hush!" He opened the door stealthily and looked out, half ran across the hall to the front door, and accompanied her into the night.

His car was waiting at the end of the drive, he told her.

"I'll make some excuse to come up to town. Take the car as far as Wimbledon station, where you can get a cab. Millie, you don't mean all you've said? You wouldn't send an old pal to the Moor—"

"I'd be glad to send you there!" She spat the words at him. "And you'll be glad if I have the chance."

"What do you mean?" he asked.

"What do I mean?" She thrust her face almost into his. "If John Leslie gets to know first, you'll be in hell to-night!"

CHAPTER XXII

MR. JOSHUA COLLIE went back to his office early in the evening, and Field literally fell upon his neck under the mistaken impression that the reporter had brought with him sufficient copy to enliven the early edition. But as he knew his Collie well, he should have realized that that was a most unlikely possibility. For Collie was one of those peculiar men, not uncommon in Fleet Street, who loved the collection of news and loathed setting it down in black and white. It was almost as though they were parting with a cherished secret. Not until the last minute of the last hour would Collie ever write a line, though his overcoat pocket was crammed with odd scraps of memoranda which nobody but he could read.

When Mr. Field had completely exhausted himself:

"A newspaper story," said Joshua oracularly, "is like a jigsaw puzzle. One may put together odd sections; one may even get a faint resemblance to the design; but until all the pieces are in place—"

"I don't wish to have a lecture from you on news," said the exasperated editor. "All I want from you is a story. It needn't even be spelled correctly—we keep a man in the office to attend to that; and the English may be your very own—even that matter can be put right. But we want the

175

bones and bowels of a news item that can be expanded by a more skilful hand than yours into a readable half column."

Joshua looked pained and wan.

"Not half a column, Mr. Field," he said with dignity, "but three columns! I am going to pick up the rest of this story at the Leopards Club. As you once remarked, it is a low haunt. I am an honorary member. But it is a useful low haunt; and this story is drifting that way. I don't know what is going to happen—the gift of prophecy has been denied me—but if it isn't something big, I'll eat my hat."

Field's big nose wrinkled.

"It is unnecessary for me to remind you, Mr. Collie," he said unpleasantly, "that the type of animal that eats straw is not much use in a well-conducted newspaper office. I'll accept your excuse, but I want the story here by ten. If you can't write it, 'phone it. If you can't 'phone it, I'll send a man to you wherever you are to take a dictated note. The *Megaphone*—"

"Curse the *Megaphone*!" said Joshua Collie cold-bloodedly. It was a terrible piece of bad language for him.

Now Joshua had one invaluable gift, peculiar to all good reporters: he had a nose for essentials; and so far he was satisfied that the *Megaphone*, his great rival, had not yet touched the edge of vital things.

His first visit, after leaving the *Post-Courier* building, was to Frank Sutton's office. As a rule, two or three clerks could be found working late; more especially was this likely when the financial half-year was approaching; and he was not disappointed to learn from the commissionaire on duty at the staff entrance that there were two clerks and a sub-manager working in the accounts department.

"Here, Mr. Collie," said the commissionaire, "what's this yarn about Leslie? They told me he'd been pinched—he was here this afternoon—went up to his office as large as life."

This was news to Joshua.

"How long was he in the building?" he asked.

"About half an hour, according to the sub-manager. He said he'd come to get his papers."

"Was anybody else here this afternoon?"

The timekeeper kept a diary, and from this he gleaned that Millie Trent had arrived soon after three, and that Frank Sutton himself had only just come and gone.

"Sutton?" Joshua was staggered.

"He just came in and went out," said the commissionaire.

Collie passed up the stairs and made his way to the lighted room where the clerks were at work. The sub-manager did not know him and rather resented his arrival, until he learned Joshua's connection with the press. He was, he said, working overtime, getting out the Bombay accounts. Apparently, Sutton & Company exported a very large number of second-hand motor cars to that city, and that afternoon the sub-manager in charge of the department had received specific instructions to collect every penny due to the firm, convert it into cash, and hold the result at Frank Sutton's orders.

"We sha'n't be finished till twelve," complained the man. "If Tillman had done his job, we'd have got through by ten. That fellow came in half an hour ago and went out again as cool as you like."

"Is Tillman here now?" asked Collie quickly.

"If he was here he would be working," said the other bitterly. "I told Mr. Sutton—"

"How extraordinary," interrupted Joshua sententiously, "that a man should be compelled on his very wedding day to attend to sordid business!"

Mr. Sutton had a headache, explained the sub-manager—he was subject to such disorders. In his office he had a small locked medicine cupboard, and this contained powders of a peculiarly potent character.

"I must say I learned more about the governor to-night than I have ever known," said the sub-manager. "He was quite chatty. I suppose you've come up to get a few items about Leslie?"

In truth, Joshua had come with no such intention, but he accepted this ready-made explanation. For the moment, he confessed, he was terribly concerned about Frank

Sutton's headaches. He could imagine no worse start for a honeymoon.

"I didn't know that he had 'em till he told me," said the sub-manager—and this was exactly what Mr. Collie wished to learn.

The manager talked about Sutton: his unfailing kindness, his courtesy and consideration for the staff.

"Leslie was a brute compared with him," he said. "The girls who work in the office have a little club—a sort of club—to buy flowers for his desk. They're always doing something for his office—pen-wipers and things."

Collie had never seen Mr. Sutton's private office. He gave the sub-manager the impression that a view of this holy of holies was necessary for an article he intended writing.

"In these days of labour troubles," he said, "the world cannot know too much about the employer who treats his staff like human beings."

He even suggested that it might be necessary to secure a photograph of the room which contained such a paragon among employers.

"You'll get me hung," said the sub-manager, taking his keys from his pocket. He conducted Mr. Collie down the dark corridor and opened a door at the end.

It was a very pleasant room, the chief feature of which was a large and handsome writing desk. A rich-looking square of carpet covered the greater expanse of the floor, and just

179

behind Sutton's padded desk chair was a small mahogany
cabinet fixed to the wall by brackets. Joshua took a leisurely
survey of the apartment, noted the handsome fireplace,
the deep armchairs, the quality of the velvet curtains that
flanked each window. Absent-mindedly he tried the door of
the cabinet, but it was locked.

"Don't touch anything, old man," begged the sub-
manager.

"A very tidy office and spotlessly clean," murmured
Joshua. "A palace!"

The desk was clear and, save for a screwed-up piece
of white paper, the waste-paper basket was empty. But the
reporter saw that on the paper was a red seal... just a glimpse
he had of the cracked and broken sealing-wax, and guessed
that Mr. Sutton must have opened a new box of powders
and thrown away the wrapping. And Joshua was anxious to
know the nature of this magic specific.

"How do those curtains draw?" he asked.

The manager showed him, concealed in the folds of the
velvet, a long silk cord. One pulled at this—he performed
the action—and the curtains covered the windows. Before
he returned his full attention to the visitor, the waste-paper
basket was empty and the paper was added to the confusion
in Mr. Collie's overcoat pocket.

He left the sub-manager in his room and went on his
way down the corridor toward the stairs. Presently he came

to the entrance to Leslie's room, stopped, and tried the door. To his surprise, it was unlocked. But he had a greater surprise still when he switched on the light. The fireplace was full of burned and charred papers, and not only was the safe door open, but the key was still in the lock.

"Dear me!" said Joshua.

He peered into the safe: it was entirely empty. Not so much as a sheet of paper was left of its contents. The three shelves were bare. Thoughtfully, he closed the safe, locked the door, and put the key on Leslie's table. Somebody intended to make a very quick get-away, and was destroying—what?

He poked among the ashes, found nothing, until at the very bottom were two half sheets of typewritten paper, the greater part of which had been burned away. The first of these read:

John Leslie, an ex-convict in the em...
behaving suspiciously for a lon...
diamond collar the property of L...
safe in his office.

The second sheet was almost identical, but in both there were certain typewriting errors. He folded these sheets carefully and put them in his pocket.

This, then, was the home of The Squealer; for Elford on one occasion had, by special permission of Barrabal, shown him one of the typical squeals that The Squealer was in the habit of sending to Scotland Yard and to the Divisional Inspector of the district.

He looked up at the clock; there was time for him to eat his dinner—Joshua hated being hurried over meals—before he began the wearisome task of beginning a story which so far had no end. Most fervently, Mr. Joshua Collie prayed for a quick development, for the *Megaphone* was getting on his nerves.

There is a tiny restaurant at the back of the Empire Theatre which was a favourite haunt of the reporter's. Here, relieved of his overcoat, he sat down and relaxed with the happy sense of comforts to come.

And then he remembered Mr. Sutton's headache powders and went out to the microscopic vestibule to search his coat pocket.

He found what he was seeking and brought it back to his table.

As he straightened out the paper, he saw that the sub-manager had been mistaken—the shape was not of a carton but of a small phial. On the paper was printed the trade mark of a manufacturing chemist and the name of the drug. Beneath was the warning "Poison!"

Joshua really did whistle, for this compound name was that of one of the most powerful narcotics known to medical science. It was a drug greatly favoured by a certain type of desperate criminal who called it "The New Knock," for its effects were more drastic than the knock-out drop of old.

The waiter brought the soup as Joshua rose from the table.

"Leave it there," he said, and went out to find a telephone.

There were many eminent physicians who would go a long way to oblige Joshua Collie. The first he called was out, but at the second attempt he found himself connected with one of the brightest lights that illuminate Harley Street.

"Collie speaking—*Post-Courier*. I want to ask you what would be the effect of this drug?" He repeated the name on the paper and heard the doctor laugh.

"What is this—a new crime you've unearthed, Joshua? What would be the effect?"

"It is odourless and tasteless. If you took half a teaspoonful you would feel absolutely no effect until you made a sudden movement—lifted your hand or turned your head rather quickly. Then you would go out as though you had been hit on the head with an iron bar, and you might sleep for hours—and you'd be rather sorry for yourself when you woke up! Why do you want to know?"

"I am writing an article," said Joshua mendaciously. "It is to be called 'Should Brides Be Poisoned?'"

CHAPTER XXIII

WHEN Beryl Sutton left the drawing room and passed up the stairs, her first intention was to go to her room, and, locking the door, wait until she had brought her mind to normality. Her head was aching; a curious weakness made her knees give under her. As she entered her room, she thought she heard Lew's voice calling her from below, but purposely did not answer. Closing the door softly, she was about to lock it when a thought occurred to her. She had one hour at the most—one hour of loneliness; the last hour, perhaps, she could call her own.

Leading from her bedroom was a small dressing room, and she had made this into a cosy cubbyhole, infinitely less comfortable than her own sitting room, but having the inestimable advantage of seclusion.

Here was a long and luxurious settee, and, closing and locking first the door and then the baize inner door, she collapsed into the soft couch, and, burying her head in the cushions, strove with all her will power to compose her mind.

John Leslie was free... and she was married. In an hour, two hours, she would be on her way to Scotland with Frank Sutton.... She was Mrs. Frank Sutton. She repeated the words a dozen times, trying to take hold of the reality. But her mind refused to be disciplined. She was married, and yet she was not married. And somewhere out there beyond the dark garden the man she loved was waiting, with a heart as empty as hers.

She tried to rouse herself, to make the effort of walking to the window and looking out. Perhaps she could see him. But she was curiously lethargic; could not bring herself to move. The very weariness of death was upon her; she was striving toward oblivion, and presently oblivion came, and she fell into a dreamless sleep.

She did not even hear Lew's voice calling her from the bedroom, or the whir of car wheels....

It was the patter of rain against the window that woke her, and she sat up with a start. The room was dark, but it had been dark when she came in. She had had to feel her way to the couch. How long had she slept? It seemed incredible that she had slept at all.

She rose stiffly and shivered, for she was chilled. Feeling along the wall, she found the electric switch and pressed it, and the room was flooded with soft light. On her desk was a tiny French clock, and the hands pointed to a quarter to eleven.

A quarter to eleven! Her train left King's Cross at twenty past ten. She picked up the little clock and pressed it to her ear: it was going. And then she glanced at the watch on her wrist: it was the same hour. What had happened?

185

She went into the bedroom, turned on the light, and, opening the door, stepped on to the landing. She heard the footman talking to one of the servants below.

"...I didn't see her go. She was wearing a hat when I saw her last... he's like a lunatic. Perhaps he thinks she's gone after that fellow."

She thought it was the moment to call down the stairs, and heard a startled expression.

"Is that you, miss? Good Lord, you've given us all a fright, miss!"

She went halfway down the dark stairs.

"What has happened? Where is Mr. Friedman?"

"I don't know, miss. I think he's gone out after you." He was rather embarrassed.

"Perhaps she went after that fellow," she repeated to herself—who the fellow was to whom he was referring, she could guess.

"Mr. Friedman thought I'd gone out? Has he telephoned?"

"No, miss."

The grandfather clock in the hall struck the three quarters at that moment.

"Is that a quarter to eleven?"

"Yes, miss. All your trunks went on to the station hours ago."

The footman was anxious for further information at first hand, but she was not to be provoked into satisfying his curiosity.

"I didn't know what to do with your suitcases, miss."

Her two suitcases were strapped in the hall, waiting, she saw. She stood, one hand on the balustrade, looking down at them thoughtfully.

"Has Mr. Sutton been back?"

"No, miss—ma'am." He remembered her changed status.

"Mr."—here she hesitated—"Leslie?"

"No, miss, he hasn't come either. In fact, nobody's here except the servants." A pause. "Shall I telephone for a taxi, miss?"

"Why?"

Evidently there was reason in the footman's question. Her place was by her husband's side—how very trite that sounded! She had heard such a phrase in a play that had not been very successful, and for which she and Lew had had first-night tickets.

"Yes, please," awkwardly. "I think you had better get a taxi. The cars have gone?"

"Yes, miss, there are no cars here except your little two-seater."

Obviously, he dismissed the possibility of her using this. A lady going to Scotland on her honeymoon might find a two-seater an embarrassing possession by the time she reached King's Cross station. But, to his surprise, she jumped at the suggestion.

"Yes, please," she said eagerly. "Will you get it out for me?"

The footman was a motor cyclist and had some knowledge of cars. In ten minutes, he brought the little machine to the portico.

"I've put up the hood and the side curtains, miss—ma'am," he said. "It's raining cats and dogs. If I were you, I should wear something warm."

She smiled at this.

"You feel you stand *in loco parentis*, Robert?" she said. The gaiety in her voice was infectious, though the reason for her sudden happiness was difficult to analyze. Not so difficult, perhaps, if she allowed herself to think honestly. She was happy because she had lost the train to Scotland. Whatever happened, that journey would be postponed till—to-morrow, probably.

"If Mr. Friedman rings up, you must tell him I went to sleep in my dressing room and that I'm terribly sorry; and you can tell Mr. Sutton the same. And, Robert, tell Mr. Friedman that I am driving up to London—"

Here she stopped. Why was she driving to London? She must at least be honest with herself. She was going to Leslie, to find him. And what would happen after that, she did not know—cared less. Only she wanted to be—some place where Frank Sutton could not find her. No longer did she fret at the thought of hurting Lew. She was comfortably selfish. All the world for the moment revolved about her own happiness, her own emotions.

She must be still asleep in a moral sense, she thought, as she climbed into the car and sent the machine spinning along the London road. For even the drive of rain and the chill of the night could not wake her to the cold ugliness of duty. Her duty was to herself. Intruding on this feverish light-headedness of hers was the knowledge of one inexplicable problem that remained unsolved. Lew and duty had gone by the board. Frank was an inconsiderable factor—or would be if she could make up her mind just how she felt toward him.

If she hated him, her action was logical; if she liked him enough to be sorry for him, she would not dare think of him. But she neither liked nor hated him. He was one with Tillman—Collie—a dozen people she could recall. An interesting person to whom she was attached by no bond which could not be snapped without a pang.

In this mood Beryl Sutton came to London.

Her car came to a halt before the rather gloomy Bloomsbury house in which John Leslie had his lodgings. Exactly what she was going to do, she had no idea. What would be the outcome of her visit, she did not think or care.

As she drew nearer and nearer to London, her spirits, for some unaccountable reason, rose higher. She had money with her, and if necessary she would spend that night at a hotel. One resolution she had reached—she would not return to Wimbledon and to Frank Sutton.

The Bloomsbury boarding house had a butler who was also a part proprietor. He shook his head when she told him of her quest.

"Captain Leslie very seldom comes here except to sleep," he said, to her surprise. "I haven't seen him since Wednesday."

"Didn't he sleep here last night?" she asked.

"Not for two or three nights, miss."

"But what do you do with his letters when they come?"

"They don't come," he smiled blandly.

She heard the news in consternation. At least she had expected to find Leslie; never doubted that her first objective would be reached.

"He is working at Sutton & Co. I can give you the address."

"Thank you, I know it," she said hurriedly. "Perhaps he has gone back there."

And though it was very unlikely, she could but inquire. When she arrived, the commissionaire could only tell her what he had told "a newspaper reporter."

"Mr. Collie?" she said quickly.

Here was one who might help her, and it was strange that she had never thought of him. She did not go into the office, but turned her car Citywards, and ten minutes later Field was interviewing her in the waiting room of the *Post-Courier*.

"Miss Stedman?" he said when he came in. "You're not the lady who was married today?"

"Yes, I am," she nodded, a little subdued, "but I'm not quite used to my new name."

"I'm afraid Collie is out," said Field gently. He was a man with an eye for beauty, despite his grizzled hair and his years; for news editors are sometimes human. "I don't know where you could find him, unless..." He shook his head dubiously. "He's probably at a club, rather a low place called the Leopards, and I shouldn't advise you to go there, Mrs. Sutton. I'll 'phone him."

He went out and was gone five minutes.

"He's not there yet," he reported, "but, if you keep in touch with the office, we can let you know where he is to be found."

She was in a dilemma. Collie only had one value to her: he might be able to lead her to John Leslie. Perhaps Field knew, but he shook his head when she put the question.

"No, I only know what's in the newspaper, that he was arrested to-day. Is he a friend of yours, Mrs. Sutton?"

"Yes," she said in a low voice, "a very great friend."

"He was released on bail. That's remarkable. Barrabal's doing—though why Barrabal should let him out—"

And then, remembering that while he was speaking of a desperate criminal, he was also speaking of her friend, he endeavoured to turn the conversation, only to find himself in deeper waters.

"I shouldn't be surprised if you found Leslie at the club. They have some queer members—"

He floundered here, but she was not thinking of deplorable characters. The possibility that she might find him at this place made her heart leap.

"Could I leave my car here? I saw a lot of machines standing by the sidewalk unattended."

Mr. Field made inquiries by telephone and found that the car could be left. She had made up her mind. After seeing the machine sandwiched in a side street between two newspaper vans, she went up to Fleet Street, found a taxi, and gave the driver instructions.

"The Leopards Club, miss?" The taxi driver was staggered. "Very good."

"Do you know where it is?"

"Yes, miss, I know where it is, and I know *what* it is," grinned the taxi man. "All right, miss."

It was raining so heavily that she was already wet to the skin, but this she did not notice. The cab passed through

Kingsway, and after a while pulled up at the entrance of a narrow street. Through the rain-blurred window, she saw two men running, and heard, above the rumble and rattle of the taxi, a police whistle blow shrilly. And then she was stricken with a horrible feeling of apprehension. Flinging open the door of the cab, she jumped out.

"Wait for me!" she called over her shoulder, and fled down the narrow street.

Where the Leopards Club was, she did not know. Only she could see a crowd running and knew something awful had happened. Above the patter of flying footsteps came that nerve-shattering police whistle.

And then somebody caught her by the arm and swung her round, and she looked up into the lean face of Tillman.

"Where are you going, Miss Stedman?" he asked roughly.

She stared at him wildly.

"I don't know. Something has happened..." She could hardly find breath to speak.

"Something's happened all right. You'd better go away."

Two policemen came flying past at a run. She saw ahead of them a little knot of people gathered round the door of a building. And then somebody began screaming horribly. She put her hands to her ears to shut out the sound.

Tillman relaxed his grip on her arm for a moment, and then, obeying an impulse, she ran forward. She heard him call her back, but she took no notice. Now she was on the edge of the little crowd and saw the struggling, screaming woman whom two policemen were carrying from the building.

It was Millie Trent!

"Murder, murder!" she was screaming. "He's dead!... Leslie murdered him!"

Beryl sank back, would have collapsed, but Tillman's strong arm was round her.

Dead? Frank Sutton was dead. Instinctively she knew that she, the bride of a few hours, was a widow. John Leslie had kept his promise.

CHAPTER XXIV

THE Leopards Club figured from time to time in the police-court news, but lately a wave of respectability had come over that dubious establishment. For a year it had become something of a fashionable resort in the sense that daring young bloods who wished to show their quivering womenfolk a view of the under life of London were wont to engage a table at the Leopards and to spend a precarious night dancing to the strains of the saxophone, fiddle, and trap drum which composed the Leopards Club orchestra.

It was situate, as so many clubs of its kind are placed, on the top floor of a large building off Shaftesbury Avenue, and was registered as a social and luncheon club. Besides the cramped dining room with its still more cramped dancing floor, there were supper rooms where the members could entertain their guests privately.

Mr. William Anerley, both proprietor and commissionaire, called the largest of these latter "the board room," and suggested, both by printed notice affixed to the Club board and by advertisement, that it might be hired by directors of public meetings. There is no record that this invitation had ever been accepted.

Queer things happened at the Leopards, but the really queer things which interested the police were most rigorously prohibited. You might not drink in forbidden hours, or play, to the knowledge of the proprietor, a game less innocuous than solo whist. That members came to the club with "a shoe in their pocket," and more exciting games than auction bridge were played, not only in the board room, a favourite rendezvous, but in the smaller apartments, was fairly certain. But Bill Anerley could point with virtuous pride to certain minutes of his committee wherein was recorded the expulsion of Joe Greel and Harry Manx, who had transgressed the rules.

The committee was properly constituted, but since it had a habit of meeting at an hour in the morning when most of its members were in bed, and one of the rules of its constitution stipulated that two might form a quorum, the business of the Leopards was conducted by Mr. Anerley and his gawky son, Jim, who, in moments when he was free from the arduous business of committeeman, manipulated the lift by which the members and their friends entered the club.

Bill had no illusions about the character of the establishment or the standing of its members: and once, when he had ostentatiously struck from the roll of membership a gentleman who had brought a pigeon to be plucked, he had stated his conviction in a few pungent words.

"Do you call this a gentleman's club?" demanded the disgruntled member.

Big Bill looked at him with a cold blue eye.

"If it was a gentleman's club, Harry, your name wouldn't be on the books."

Once Jim asked him, in a slack period of the year, where the members went in the holiday season. Bill did not raise his eyes from the book where he was entering up certain charges.

"Some of 'em go to the Lydo, my boy, and some of 'em go to Ostend, and some of 'em go to Dartmoor. It all depends on what they do for a living."

A hard-faced, big-jawed man, there was only one tender spot in his composition, and that, curiously enough, was an affection for two men, one of whom was entirely unknown to him.

It was a favourite story of Bill's, that he told the interested Jim in slack moments.

"He used to call me 'Percy.' I met him first in a shell hole the other side of Hill 60, and we lay there for three days. He was an officer and I was a private... and he used to call me Percy. 'Hullo, Percy,' he used to say, when a shell came over. 'That one nearly got you!' He tied up my leg and kept me alive with water that he ought to have been drinking hisself. I'd give a thousand pound to meet him. If I could have only got down from the bus in time that day..."

He referred to a memorable afternoon in July when he and Jim were taking a blow on the top of a bus. As they had passed Piccadilly Circus, Bill had recognized his hero and

197

signalled frantically to him, without attracting attention, and, descending in haste, had made a vain search. Piccadilly is a place of great activity, and the unknown had vanished.

As to the other, he never spoke of him at all, but there is little he would not have done for the financier who at a critical period had established Bill Anerley as the proprietor of The Club. For Mr. Lewis Friedman he had a profound respect—for the unknown officer something of veneration.

It was nine o'clock and a very quiet night—so quiet that Anerley the younger had been given the earlier part of the evening off to go to the pictures. He returned to find his father a very thoughtful man.

There had been some trouble with the orchestra, and Bill had substituted an electrically propelled gramophone in the dancing room, and the squeak and squall of it came at intervals as the door was opened.

"Anybody in the ballroom to-night, Father?" Jim, in an ill-fitting uniform, lounged against the entrance of the lift.

"Nobody to-night, my boy," said Bill, looking over his pince-nez. His own commissionaire's uniform was a gorgeous thing of gold and mulberry. "And I wish, my boy, you'd get out of the habit of asking questions."

Jim sighed. He was young, and excitement was his normal fare.

"Couldn't we do something to liven things up?" he asked.

His father looked at him sternly.

"What do you mean—buy a couple of toy balloons and call it a gala dance?" he demanded sardonically. "No, Jim, there's nothing to worry about. Everybody's out of town."

The telephone bell on his desk rang. He took down the receiver. It was an inquiry from an agitated lady.

"No, Mrs. Lattit, your husband isn't here... no, he hasn't been in the club to-day—I haven't seen him, at any rate. Yes, Mrs. Lattit, I'll tell him."

He put down the receiver, rang a bell, and a little waiter appeared.

"Go and tell Mr. Lattit his wife's asking after him," he said. "He's in Number Four—no, no, Number Three. Don't go disturbing Number Four—he's having a sleep."

"Who's that?" asked Jim.

Mr. Anerley adjusted his glasses, unnecessarily, for he looked over them at the youth.

"Who's what?" he demanded.

"Who's in Number Four?"

"Mr. Albert Alfred Henry John Jones," said Bill. "He lives at 906 Nowhere Court."

Jim was crushed to silence. Presently his father enlightened him.

"If you want to know, it's one of the members who wants to keep out of sight. And if you ask what you're to say if the police inquire about him, I'll give you a thick ear!"

199

Jim was saved the trouble of a retort. The lift bell rang, and he descended. He was back again in a minute and ushered the visitor into the corridor.

"Good-evening, Mr. Sutton."

Bill favoured the newcomer with a glance that was meant to be gracious; for Sutton, if he was not a frequent, was a generous, patron of the club. He looked round now at the waiting boy, and Bill, taking the hint, gave his son a signal to make himself scarce—a simple matter for a lift attendant.

Until the whine of the descending elevator ceased, Sutton did not speak, and his shrewd observer realized that the request to be made of him was of a special character, for it was not unusual for Mr. Frank Sutton to require a special service. There was an occasion when Bill had arranged one of the private rooms in such a manner that Sutton could interview a caller without his identity being revealed or his face seen by the visitor.

Bill Anerley never inquired too closely into the profession or the occupation of his members. The club, he often said, was for service. He had adopted this phrase bodily from the advertisement of a well-known trading house.

But it sounded fine, and, in a sense, went to the salving of his conscience.

Sutton was no favourite of his, but he was a man of wealth, a generous paymaster, and, as such, to be treated with respect.

"I want a room. Is the board room vacant?"

"Yes, sir," said Bill. "Are you expecting somebody?"

His hand was halfway to the bell when the other stopped him. In turning, he knocked against the visitor, and Frank Sutton cursed him and felt gingerly at his arm.

"It is all right," he said, with a wince of pain, "but I was in a motor-car accident the other night and cut myself rather badly."

Bill was all apologies, but these Sutton cut short.

"You needn't let the waiters in on this," he said. "I'd like you to look after the matter yourself. I want a couple of pints of champagne, two glasses, and no interruption."

This in itself was not a remarkable request.

"A lady, Mr. Sutton?"

Frank Sutton nodded thoughtfully.

"Yes—you know her: she's been here before with me."

"Miss Trent?" Bill was interested.

"Yes, Miss Trent."

There was something else coming. Bill knew that the really important communication was as yet unmade. Sutton would not have sent the boy out of the way to order a couple of pints of champagne and a private room.

201

The big corridor was quiet; only the faint strains of the gramophone came from the dance room, where three lonely couples were endeavouring to work up a spurious gaiety.

"The fact is, Bill, I'm in a frightful mess."

Bill inclined his head graciously. Most of his clients, at some time or other, were in a frightful mess; and not once but many times had he been called upon to extricate them from unhappy and complicated situations. Yet he could not help wondering why a man of Mr. Frank Sutton's undoubted wealth and influence should find himself in a difficulty, unless—

He had had the faintest of hints that Sutton's business was not altogether straight. There had been occasions when this prosperous merchant had held conferences in the board room with men whom Anerley knew to be expert jewel thieves. Was it a police matter? he wondered.

"I'll tell you the facts," said Sutton. "I've had a little tiff with our friend—you're a man of the world, Anerley, and you understand what I mean."

A tiff, to Bill, meant anything from a mild argument to a stand-up fight.

"The truth is," said Sutton, "I was married to-day."

"Oh!" said Bill, genuinely astonished.

"And Miss Trent, who has been a very good friend of mine, has taken it rather badly. I'm leaving for Scotland to-night, and she's threatened to come down to the station and make a scene. Well, you realize what that means."

"She ought to be sensible," said Bill, shaking his head, reproving the absent Millie. "I'm quite sure a gentleman like you could easily square the thing. A few hundred pounds—"

"Money isn't in question," said the other impatiently. "You don't understand. I've discovered that, unfortunately, for some reason or other, Miss Trent has become violently attached to me. You understand what I mean?"

"I understand," said Bill, wondering what was coming next. Was he expected to placate the enraged Millie? he wondered. Apparently not.

"She will be coming here in a quarter of an hour," Sutton went on, "and I am going to have a little talk with her. After I've gone"—he paused, and looked Bill straight in the eyes—"she will probably have a little sleep. I don't want her to be disturbed before tomorrow morning—say, four o'clock."

CHAPTER XXV

NOW Bill Anerley understood and shook his head.

"That's a bit too dangerous, Mr. Sutton," he said. "I can't afford to take the risk. Suppose she starts a squeal, what will I look like?"

Sutton's eyes did not waver.

"Suppose somebody else starts a squeal?" he said slowly. "I don't see that you're responsible for anything I do; and it isn't the first time that people have wakened up in this club with a headache."

"It will be the first woman that's wakened up in this club with a headache," said Bill coolly. "I'm sorry, it can't be done."

"It can't, eh? Then what will happen when I've gone and you find the lady sleeping? Will you send for the police? I don't think so, Bill. I needn't have told you anything about it. If I'd walked out and left her there and told you I was coming back in an hour or two, you'd have made no trouble."

"I can't have anybody doped in this club," said Bill doggedly; "but if she's going to make a fuss—well, I can understand how you feel about it, Mr. Sutton."

Sutton took a pad of notes from his pocket, detached three and laid them on the desk.

"And of course," said Bill, his eyes on the money, "if it's not going to hurt her..."

He gathered the notes mechanically, folded them, and slipped them into his pocket.

"When will you be back?" he asked, as Sutton rang the lift bell.

"Either before or after her. Show her into the board room, if that's vacant."

Bill nodded.

"If she comes before me, tell her I sha'n't be very long."

After Sutton had gone, Bill climbed on to the high stool behind his desk and ran his fingers through his gray hair. Jim returned to find him glaring at the book before him.

"What's the matter, Father?"

"Eh?... Nothing," said Bill roughly. "Don't ask questions."

"What's that fellow do for a living—that Mr. Sutton?"

"He's a gentleman," snarled Bill.

He roused himself with an effort, got down from his stool, and, going into the little wine bar, found a bottle of champagne, put it on a tray with glasses and a small silver box of biscuits, and brought it to the board room: a large, rather gaudily decorated apartment. He switched on the lights, took a look round, and put a light to the gas stove. Outside, he saw a waiter and beckoned him.

"Somebody's coming here. You needn't dodge in or dodge out. And, Adolf—after this gentleman's gone, I don't want you to go into the room to clear up—do you understand?"

"*Oui, monsieur.*"

'When I say I don't want you to go into the room to clear up," said Bill, the advisability of clearing himself from any responsibility occurring to him, "I merely mean that the gentleman has hired the room till closing time."

"*Oui, monsieur,*" said Adolf, who was not unused to receiving mysterious orders. "Also in Number Four—"

"He's asleep—I told you that!" snapped Bill. "You're not to disturb him. Anybody who wants in this club can sleep just as long as he dam' pleases."

Bill went back to his high desk and leaned upon its side.

"I often wonder, Jim," he said, with gentle melancholy, "what He would say if he knew I was running this kind of show."

"Gawd?" asked Jim, pardonably deceived by the reverent pronunciation of the pronoun.

"You know who I'm talking about," said his father testily; "the chap that used to call me Percy."

"Perhaps he's dead," said Jim. "A lot of fellows got killed in the war."

Bill eyed him malignantly.

There was the sound of angry voices from behind a curtained doorway that led to the private rooms. A tall youth in evening dress, rather flushed of face and wild of hair, came out, followed by a thickset man.

"Hi, hi, what's the trouble?" asked Bill sternly.

There was really no need for him to ask: he could guess. Walters, the nimble-fingered, and his confederate had been "entertaining" young Mr. Weatherby for the past hour.

"This young swine " began Walters truculently.

"You pulled a card out of your pocket—I saw you!" roared the youth, and Walters drew back his arm.

"Steady!" Bill's voice had the quality of steel.

"I'll break his—"

"Oh, will you?" Bill Anerley's smile was entirely mirthless. "You don't do any breaking here, Walters."

"Well, what's he mean by accusing me?" demanded the stout man.

Bill ignored him.

"How much have you lost, sir?" he asked the youth.

"Twenty-five pounds. I don't mind that—"

"You've lost twenty-five pounds." Bill held out his hand to the scowling Walters. "Cough up," he said laconically.

"What do you mean?" demanded the man.

"I'm telling yer!" Bill Anerley's voice rose to a roar, and most reluctantly and slowly Walters put his hand in his pocket, produced five notes, and passed them to Bill, who examined them critically. He handed one back.

"Snide," he said.

"Eh?" said Walters innocently.

"Slush. Don't let's have any argument."

Walters replaced the counterfeit note.

"There you are, sir." Bill folded the fivers and handed them to the ruffled loser.

"Thank you, Bill." Weatherby handed one of the notes to the commissionaire, who pocketed it and opened the lift.

"Jim, get Mr. Weatherby's hat."

There was a silence till Jim returned and the lift had carried the pigeon out of sight.

"What do you want to stick your nose in for?" growled Walters.

"Do you want to know?" asked Bill. "There's no squeal going to come from this club, see? Keep 'em quiet and we'll say nothing. Let 'em squeal and I come in."

"Give me back that fiver he gave you," demanded Walters, and Bill's laughter filled the corridor.

"I'll give you a punch on the nose, that's what I'll give you," he said calmly, and provoked the inevitable query:

"Is this supposed to be a gentlemen's club? I'll report you to the committee."

"I'm the committee," said Bill, and crooked his finger. "Come here." And, as though fascinated by a snake, Walters obeyed. "Go back and have your drink," said Bill with ominous quiet. "Argue with me and I'll drop you down that lift and break your perishing neck!"

Walters slouched back to his private room and his companions.

"Nice club, I must say!" he grumbled.

"It's the only club you'll ever be a member of, except the Pentonville Old Boys," said Bill.

Jim had hurried back that he might be a spectator of a scene that he had witnessed so often but that he never failed to enjoy. He came back, too, with a piece of information.

"Dad, you know that gentleman you pointed out from the top of the 'bus—that officer, the one you were talking about just now

Bill took off his glasses and laid them on the desk.

"Yes; what about him?"

"I saw him just now," said Jim.

Bill's jaw dropped.

"You never did?"

"I did."

"Where?"

"Just outside the door."

Bill Anerley shook his head contemptuously.

"Not you!"

209

"I did, I tell you," insisted Jim. "He was standing on the other side of the road when I took that young swell down. I had a good look at him, and I was just going across the road to talk to him when he turned and walked off."

Bill stared at his progeny.

"What would you have said to him?"

"I'd have said: 'Are you the gentleman who saved my old man's life? If you are, do you mind popping up in the lift and seeing him?"

"'Popping up in the lift'!" wailed Bill scornfully. "There's manners! After the money I've spent on your education!" He eyed his son dubiously. "It wasn't him. You didn't see him properly that day on the 'bus."

"I saw him plain."

"He's good-looking," said Bill, "so you couldn't have seen him. I wish I could meet him again." He shook his head. "How was he dressed?"

Jim considered this point.

"He had gray hair," he said.

"Did he wear any trousers?" demanded his father sarcastically.

"I mean, his hair was gray. He wore a sort of dark suit and a gray hat."

Bill shook his head again.

"That's how he was dressed when I saw him. No, it wasn't him."

210

And then he smiled reminiscently.

"You know the last thing he said to me was: 'Percy, if we ever get out of this, we'll have a good dinner at the Carlton.'"

Jim didn't know the Carlton. Was it the hotel next to Lyons'? His father snorted.

"You lower everything you touch," he said. "You'd lower this club, only it couldn't be any lower."

The lift bell rang. Jim made a dive down to bring the newcomer. At the sight of him Bill grinned uneasily.

Mr. Collie was not a frequent visitor to the Leopards Club; there was something of a stormy petrel about this amiable man, and it was Bill Anerley's experience that the reporter of the *Post-Courier* never put in an appearance unless there was trouble in the offing. He was an honorary member, as he was of most clubs of this character. Bill's motto was "Keep in with the press," for he had the delusion that there might come a time when all the majesty and machinery of Fleet Street would turn to extricate him from some unhappy situation.

"Good-evening, Mr. Collie," he said, as he shook hands. "This is a sight for sore eyes. I haven't seen you for years. I often read the bits you put in the paper."

Mr. Collie surveyed him gravely.

"I thought you were looking a little more intellectual than when I saw you last. Dear me, the old place hasn't changed," he said, looking round. He touched the wall. "I remember that beer stain. Who was it threw the bottle at you?"

Bill grinned politely at the age-old joke, and then, confidentially:

"I say, Mr. Collie—nothing doing, is there?"

Collie shook his head.

"I know that you gentlemen get about among the 'busies.'"

But apparently Joshua Collie's complete attention was concentrated upon the garnishings of this unsavoury little dive.

"You've had the carpet beaten," he said. "It wasn't like that three years ago." And then: "Is anybody here?"

"No one you know, Mr. Collie. Are you expecting anybody?"

Collie looked up at the ceiling and rubbed his chin.

"Well—er—no, and yes. If my office calls me up, will you tell them that I'm ... you know?"

Bill knew.

"You're not here? All right, sir. Do you want a room?"

The need for a room had evidently not occurred to Joshua, for he had to consider the matter for some moments. Bill often used to wonder what this cherubic old man thought about in those long, silent pauses of his. Joshua, at the moment, was wondering whether the cost of a room at the Leopards Club might be properly included in his expense account, and decided that it might be.

"Yes, I think I'll have a room."

Bill pushed the bell.

"You're all alone, Mr. Collie?" he asked waggishly.

"I hope so," said Collie in haste. "And if there are any riotous parties here, I should like to be put a long way from them."

The waiter appeared in the curtained doorway.

"Mr. Collie in 9. Is there anything you want?"

Joshua thought he would like beer and solitude, and then, as a thought struck him:

"Is there a Mr. Tillman a member of this club?"

Bill frowned, reached out for a membership book, and ran his finger down the page.

"No, sir."

"Thank God for that!" sighed Mr. Collie piously.

CHAPTER XXVI

FATHER and son watched the shuffling figure of the reporter till he disappeared.

"He doesn't often come here, does he, Dad?" asked Jim.

Bill shook his head.

"No. When he does there's trouble." He looked at his watch. "Go and take a screw outside. I wonder where that Sutton's gone to?"

Even as he spoke, the lift bell rang, and in a few seconds Sutton stepped out of the elevator, and Jim noticed that he had changed his suit.

"Has the lady come?" he asked quickly.

"No, sir."

Sutton was surprised at this.

"She hasn't come?"

Bill lowered his voice.

"You want to be very careful about the other matter, sir."

"You mean the sleep? Don't worry about that."

Bill shrugged.

"All right, sir, it's your funeral. You haven't said anything to me—I don't know anything about it at all."

"That's all right," said Sutton. "There's another thing, Anerley—do you know Captain Leslie?"

Bill shook his head.

"No, sir."

"Isn't he a member?"

"No, sir; we've got lots of captains but no Leslies."

Sutton considered this for a time.

"It's very likely that his name isn't Leslie at all; in fact, it's pretty certain that it's something else and that he's given this name."

"Most of our members aren't captains either. Who is he, sir?"

Apparently Sutton did not hear this, and he repeated the question.

"Leslie? Oh, he's an old lag," he said, and Bill chuckled.

"Well, he's qualified for membership of our little circle, anyway!" he said. "Are you expecting him?"

"Expecting him?" said Sutton slowly. "I don't know whether I am or whether I'm not. At any rate, if he comes here and inquires for me, I'm not in. Frankly, Bill, he's an enemy of mine, and he's threatened me—"

"You leave him to me, sir," said Bill confidently. "I can deal with anybody short of Dempsey. I've got an old cosh here that'd put a lion to sleep."

He whisked up his frock coat, drew a short life preserver from his trousers pocket, and thrust it in again.

"Captain Leslie... I'll remember the name. Do you want anything sir?"

It was Collie standing in the doorway. How long he had been there, Bill did not know. Following the direction of his eyes, Sutton turned, and at the sight of the reporter he gasped.

Apparently the surprise was mutual. Mr. Collie's mouth opened in a childish O.

"Isn't this the most amazing coincidence!" he said in an awe-stricken voice.

"I didn't expect to find you here," said Sutton nervously.

"I didn't expect to find myself here," said Collie, on his most genial note. "That is the peculiarity of my profession— we are always finding ourselves in the last place we expected to be!"

He wanted, he said, a little piece of wood, "about so long"—he showed the distance between two fingers—"and so wide."

Bill opened his desk and, after a search, found a small piece of wood.

"Will that do, sir?" he asked. "Did you want it for anything special?" and was staggered to learn that all these elaborate preparations were designed to remove a fly that had fallen in Mr. Collie's beer.

"He might have asked for a spoon while he was about it," smiled Bill, after the reporter had gone back to his room.

Sutton was lingering, loath to depart to the board room.

"Do you know a man named Barrabal?" he asked.

"Not Inspector Barrabal?"

Sutton nodded.

"I've heard about him."

"He's never been here, has he?"

Bill pursed his lips dubiously.

"He may have been. I shouldn't have known him. He's not a regular 'busy'—he doesn't go about much, according to accounts I hear."

After a while, Sutton passed through the doorway to his room.

Bill was troubled; he had a creepy feeling that something unusual was going to happen, and he wished Collie would come back again, or that he could find time to interview the reporter. His wish was realized, for a few minutes after Sutton had gone to his room, Collie returned, holding the piece of stick gingerly.

"What does one do with dead flies?" he asked.

217

"Give it to my boy," said Bill. "He's collecting 'em! Mr. Collie, is Mr. Sutton a friend of yours?"

Joshua was never prepared to admit that anybody was a friend of his. He replied evasively. And then he took Bill's breath away by asking:

"Have you on your list of members a Captain Leslie?"

Bill Anerley stared at him.

"That's a coincidence, Mr. Collie," he said, ""You're the second gentleman who has asked me that question."

Joshua smiled.

"The other gentleman being Mr. Sutton, of course."

"He's a lag, isn't he?" asked Bill.

"A vulgar term, but possibly that describes him. What room has Sutton got?"

But here he was asking Bill to break the one rule that was invariably observed.

"We can't tell you that. We never give particulars about members—"

"The board room," murmured Collie, and Bill was very properly nettled. "I'll go back and see what the flies have done to my beer," said the reporter.

"That's the only fly we've got!" Bill shouted after him, but the last retort was with Collie.

"If I'd known that, I'd have drunk something that wasn't poisonous," he called back from the passage.

218

The lift had gone down to the lower floor. Bill had a few minutes to himself, and took down the membership book, running his fingers down those pages devoted to the 'L's.'

"Lane, Larry, Leach, Larkley, Lando...." He shook his head. There was no Leslie. He heard the lift stop with a jerk; the door was flung open, and an excited Jim leaped out.

"It's him, guv'nor!" He was all a-twitter with excitement, pointing to the man who was emerging from the elevator.

"Him?"

And then he saw the visitor's face and went toward him with both hands outstretched.

"Why, sir, this is a wonderful sight! Don't you know me, sir, after all these years? God bless my heart, sir, I'd sooner see you than a thousand pounds!"

John Leslie frowned and shook his head.

"I don't remember you—" he began.

"Not the shell hole, sir, at the back of Hill 60?" asked Bill incredulously, and a slow smile dawned on Leslie's face.

"Good Lord—Percy!" he gasped.

"Percy!" Bill was quivering with delight. "Did you hear him, Jim—Percy!"

He was laughing, but there were tears in his eyes.

"Here, Jim, come and shake hands with the gentleman who saved your father's life."

When Jim had been pushed forward, grinning sheepishly:

"You don't know how glad I am to see you, sir! Thank Gawd, I've met you! Remember that whizz-bang coming over and saying. 'Look out, Percy! If you get to heaven first tell 'em I'm busy.'—Percy's been a sacred name to me ever since!"

Leslie was laughing softly.

"It's good to see you," he said at last. "What is your name?"

"Call me Percy, sir," begged Bill, and the other nodded.

"You're a bit older. Are you the porter of this club?"

Bill coughed; he realized the need for explaining himself away.

"Well, to tell you the truth, sir, I am the club. I bought it off an Italian—borrowed the money from a regular old swell—who got nine months for running it—the Italian, not the gentleman I'm talking about. I got the license back, and—well, it's not like the Athenaeum, you know. I've got to take a few risks, but I must live."

Leslie shook his head glumly.

"If you'd died in that shell hole, you'd have died clean," he said quietly.

"Yes, but I'd have died in debt," said Bill, who had no false sentiment. "You're not a member here, sir?"

"No, I'm not a member here," said Leslie.

"I can make you one, sir; though I think you'd better not, a gentleman like you. Might I ask your name, sir? I've often wanted to know it."

"My name is Leslie—Captain Leslie."

He saw the look of consternation that came to the man's face, and misread its cause.

CHAPTER XXVII

"CAPTAIN LESLIE?" said Bill, in an awe-stricken whisper. "But you're not the gentleman I'm thinking about? Do you know Mr. Collie?"

"The newspaper man? Yes."

Bill stared helplessly from the visitor to his son, and then:

"Jim, go downstairs." And, when the lift had gone: "I didn't want to say too much in front of him. You don't mind if I ask you something very rude—you'll excuse the liberty I'm taking?"

"Fire ahead," said Leslie, who knew what was coming.

"Somebody was talking about you to-night."

"Sutton?"

There was no mistake, then. Bill's heart, that did not ordinarily respond to human emotions, was aching. So this was Leslie—Leslie, the old lag! Leslie, nothing like the ideal he had worshipped all these years!

"I suppose he told you I was a jailbird?"

"Well, sir," said Bill disparagingly, "something like that. I'm very sorry, sir." His voice was almost tender. "You've had a bit of trouble, I suppose—we all have. I'm very sorry."

"Don't waste your sympathy on me, Percy," said Leslie cheerfully. "I'm quite happy."

222

Bill's spirits rose. That was good news. Even a respected jailbird was less preferable than one hardened in sin and ready to make a joke of his delinquencies.

"That's the way to look at life, sir: don't let your troubles get on top of you—would you like to see the club, sir? It's not much of a place. We've got as good a cellar as any you'll find in New York." He laughed. "That's a little joke, sir. They're all teetotallers in New York."

"Is Sutton in the club?" asked Leslie.

Bill might not break the rules for Mr. Collie; to tell the truth to this man was another matter.

"He's in the board room."

"The board room? Where's that? Oh, that's the corner room. I've seen a plan of the club. Is he alone?"

"With a bottle of wine, sir," said Bill. "He's expecting a lady."

Leslie nodded.

"He said he's an enemy of yours, sir." Bill dropped his voice. "He said as much. And if he's your enemy, he's my enemy!"

He pulled the life preserver from his pocket and thrust it into Leslie's hand.

"Go and cosh him!"

Leslie pushed the weapon aside.

"No, I've no particular desire to cosh him."

"Go on, sir!" urged Bill. "Tell him you've got permission from the secretary!"

"Where's Collie?"

"He's in No. 9, eating flies," said Bill recklessly.

"I'll go along and see him." Then, as Bill offered to show him the way: "All right, I'll find it without assistance."

"Excuse me, sir." Leslie turned at the door. "If there's any kind of trouble," whispered Bill, "you'll find a little service stairway right opposite the room. It leads down to the back of the house—and, sir... are you putting 'paid' to an old account?"

Leslie's face was set and hard.

"By God, I am!" he said, and the curtain he held aside dropped over him and hid him from sight.

The "sleeper" in Room Four heard him pass and opened the door a fraction of an inch to watch him. He saw Leslie pause at a room and heard Mr. Collie's surprised greeting... the door closed and the sound of their voices became a faint drone.

In the board room, Sutton waited with gathering impatience for the arrival of the woman he had summoned to meet him. Every minute was precious now. He had abandoned his intention of returning to Wimbledon, and with that change of plan he called up Lew Friedman's house. Every private room at the Leopards had a telephone connection, and he got through to Hillford almost immediately.

"Mr. Friedman's gone to town, sir—so has Miss Beryl—Mrs. Sutton," Robert's voice answered him. "No, sir... I don't know where... the trunks have gone."

He left Sutton with the impression that Lew and the girl had gone together to the station. Had he been a little less impatient, Mr. Frank Sutton might have discovered that the two people in whose movements he was interested had left Wimbledon at two hours' interval, each ignorant of the destination of the other.

("I ought to have told him that Miss Beryl's suitcases are still here," said Robert to the pretty parlourmaid.)

Sutton had opened the champagne, had filled and emptied one glass. In the other he had very carefully dropped thirty drops of a waterlike fluid from the little brown phial he produced from his waistcoat pocket. In the course of his checkered career, he had twice used "the drop," but never before had he employed more than twenty minims—this was a case where he could afford to take no risks, however.

"For luck!" he said, as he dripped the extra ten.

His visit to town that afternoon had been in connection with a change in his plans. Lew Friedman would have been a surprised man if he had realized that the hurrying on of the wedding had been determined, not by himself, but by Mr. Sutton. And it had been so ordered because he had discovered that he had mistaken the date on which the Empress of India sailed from Liverpool.

With the one man who might stop the wedding, he had effectively dealt. It was no coincidence that John Leslie had been arrested that morning. Never for one moment had Sutton dreamed of such an impossible happening as the release of Leslie on bail. At best, it would take him a fortnight to establish his innocence, and by that time Sutton hoped to be well beyond his reach.

He heard a tap at the door and looked up quickly at the empty glass, drawing it a little nearer his own, before he bade the knocker come in, though he might have known that Millie would dispense with the formality of knocking.

It was Bill Anerley, and it occurred to the visitor that the man looked ill. His moist face had a sickly pallor that was unusual.

"All right, sir?" His voice was hoarse, his manner embarrassed. He blinked amazedly at Sutton, as if he were seeing some strange spectacle.

"Why shouldn't I be all right?"

Bill did not answer.

"About the gent—fellow Leslie," he said, lowering his voice. "What have you done to him?"

It was on the point of Sutton's tongue to tell the inquirer to mind his own business, but Bill's help might be vitally necessary. Besides, it occurred to him that it was unnecessary any longer to sustain this role of successful business man. Out of his part, he was one with Anerley, except that Anerley

226

was his superior in that he did not stray far from the path of rectitude.

"I took his girl—naturally, he's sore," he said with a smile.

"Oh, you took his girl?" said Bill slowly. "I see."

He saw many possibilities: most of them were grossly unfair to the lady in question.

"Of course—that explains everything," nodded Bill.

"Explains what?" asked Sutton sharply.

"Why he wants to get you. Do you pouch a gun?"

"No," said the other, but Bill knew that he was lying.

The commissionaire's eyes roved the table. He saw the two glasses—and nodded.

"All right, sir."

He withdrew, closing the door behind him, and went in search of Leslie. But Leslie was not with the reporter, and for the moment Bill's warning must be postponed.

The man in the board room looked at his watch again and cursed softly. He took an evening newspaper from his pocket and tried to read, but he could not fix his mind upon the page. He poured out another glassful of wine as he read, and then the telephone bell rang and he snatched up the instrument. It was Millie, and his face flushed red with rage when he realized that she was not yet in the building.

"What the hell do you mean by keeping me waiting?" he asked furiously. "I'm late as it is... don't talk on the 'phone.

Come up and see me right away... Detectives be damned! They're not watching you. Where are you?"

She was at a restaurant almost opposite the club. That was better.

"Well, come up. I'm not going to talk on the 'phone. Come up—I want to see you very badly—and I've some news to give you."

He slammed down the receiver, so enraged with her that he was on the point of telling her the truth, that this time it was not to be one of those adventures of his that ended at the church door.

Never before had fate brought him so desirable a morsel as Beryl Stedman. His cabin was reserved; in an hour and a half they would be on their way to Liverpool together, and months must elapse before Lew Friedman knew the truth. It would be easy to keep him in good humour, he decided. Lew had been suspicious at the tone of Millie Trent—all that was necessary for Sutton to do was to write from the ship, telling him that he had decided upon Canada instead of Scotland because he wanted to break off his affair with his late secretary. And Millie would be sensible. He had seen her in these rages before, and it was very likely that, if she was allowed a free hand, she would come to the station and make a fuss. But in the morning... when she realized the inevitable... Frank Sutton smiled. He did not overrate the venom of a jealous woman. Millie had been that way before, with less reason. He could deal with Millie.

He raised his head. There was a murmur of men's voices outside the door of the room. They died down in an instant, and he took up the paper, trying hard to interest himself in the sporting news. He was dreading the interview, and he needed all the bracing that good wine could give him. He drank the second glass at a gulp.

He heard a noise and looked up. The door was opening slowly. A hand holding a pistol came through. He saw nothing, but that instinct which is greater than reason made him jerk his head round. For a second he stared at the bulbous muzzle of a pistol, and at the white face of the man in the doorway, and then he leapt to his feet, jerking out the automatic from his hip pocket....

He did not hear the explosion—hardly saw the red flicker of flame that came from the silencer.... Frank Sutton went down to the floor with a crash.

A little pause, and then the door of the board room opened, and John Leslie stepped in, and in his hand was the smoking pistol. He looked down at the still figure, slipped the gun into his pocket, and turned the man over. One glance at the distorted face he gave....

"Squealer," he said aloud, "you'll squeal no more!"

CHAPTER XXVIII

CAPTAIN LESLIE did not find it convenient to return by the way he had entered the building. Instead, he passed through the little service door and went down the narrow stone steps. At the bottom, an open door led him to the street. By this means he avoided meeting Millie Trent when she stepped from the elevator.

Out in the corridor, Bill Anerley had heard first a queer "plop," and then a thud.

He looked up, wiping his wet forehead with a handkerchief.

With quivering fingers, he turned the leaves of his day book. A coshing, that was all.... The captain was going to give this man a towelling. Nothing worse than that. He had stolen his girl—it was right that he should be coshed.

"Good-evening, miss." Bill's voice was husky, his face the colour of chalk.

"Where's Sutton?" asked Millie Trent.

"Sutton?" He put his trembling hand to his mouth. "You mean—Mr. Sutton?"

"You know who I mean," she said suspiciously. "What's wrong with you?"

"Nothing." Bill's voice was very loud. "I'll go along and tell him."

"Don't worry, I know the way. He's in the board room, I suppose?"

She would have passed him, but he stood in her path.

"What's the idea?" There was the slightest tremor in her voice.

"I'd better tell him you're coming," said Bill.

"Has he got somebody with him?" she asked quickly.

"No!" He almost shouted the word.

Both hands on hips, she stood surveying him and nodding slowly.

"I see. Listen, Anerley—have you had any orders about me?"

He was patently relieved even for this short respite.

"I don't know what you mean, Miss Trent," he said. "I've had no orders except to show you in."

"I mean, you haven't been told to set a bottle of wine for me, have you?"

"There's certainly a bottle of wine there," said Bill. "It would be strange if there wasn't, wouldn't it?"

She laughed harshly.

"I suppose you haven't been instructed what is to be done if you go into the board room and find me sleeping after Sutton has left, have you?" she demanded.

Bill swallowed something. The unexpectedness of the question was unnerving.

"I see. Well, I'm not going to trouble you to wake me up or to act as my little guardian angel. When Sutton goes, I'll go. That old gag!" she said contemptuously. "He thinks he's going to catch me! That's the idea, isn't it?"

"I know nothing about it," said Bill noisily. "You mustn't make accusations of that kind. This is a respectable club—"

"This is a respectable club and you know nothing about it!" she mocked him. "You wouldn't squeal if you did."

Bill stooped and thrust his big face into hers.

"If there's any squealing going to be done in this town, I reckon you and him could do it," he said meaningly.

She looked round at the lift boy.

"Who was that man you brought up some little time ago? I was watching through the window of the Barford restaurant. It was Leslie, wasn't it?"

It was Bill who answered.

"I don't know who you mean."

"You're lying," said Millie scornfully. "And here's an order to you, Bill Anerley. If I'm not out of the board room in a quarter of an hour, you ring Inspector Barrabal, and if you don't, I'll raise a squeal that'll put you out of business!"

"What a lady!" breathed Jim as she disappeared.

Bill said nothing. He was waiting... waiting. Presently came the first scream. Bill beckoned his son to him, and his voice was very husky when he gave the order which was, he knew, for his own extinction.

232

"Go down to the street, find a copper and bring him up," he said. "And if they pinch me, get away home to your mother and tell her there's nothing to be worried about. Tell her I'm 'Percy' to-night—she'll understand."

CHAPTER XXIX

WHEN Beryl came to consciousness, she was sitting in the cab. She learned afterward that the cab driver, fearful of being bilked, had followed her and helped to get her back to that vehicle. A man was standing at the open door with a glass half filled with water in his hand, and by her side sat a woman, a stranger whom she had never seen before, never saw afterward; a painted woman with sham jewellery, who was destined to come in out of the dark into her life and vanish again.

"Thank you very much; I'm all right now," Beryl gasped. Her head was whirling. "Have they—have they caught—"

"They'll never catch the murderer. He's the fellow who was arrested this morning and released on bail. I'll bet Barrabal is kicking himself now."

Who was it speaking? To her surprise, she found that it was a policeman. Even policemen can be indiscreet, and a greater indiscretion than criticizing in public a high officer of Scotland Yard, it was difficult to imagine.

"Where shall I drive you, miss?" asked the taxi man.

She tried to think. She had left her car somewhere....

"To the office of the *Post-Courier*" she said eventually.

She never saw the strange woman go, never even thanked her, and she was halfway to Fleet Street before she realized the extent of her ingratitude. Again she sent up her name, and this time Field came down to her. Before she could ask a question:

"Were you at the Leopards Club when the murder was committed?"

She shook her head.

"No—I was outside. It was dreadful!" She shuddered, and put her hand before her eyes to shut out the memory.

"You didn't see Collie?"

Again she shook her head.

"Was he there?"

"He was there all right," said Field grimly; "and if he isn't drunk and half the story he has put through on the 'phone is true, we've got the biggest story that has ever been published in my time. Did you see Barrabal—do you know him?"

"The police officer? No," she said. "The only person I knew was a man called Tillman—"

"Oh!" He looked at her oddly. "You saw Tillman, did you? Humph! He was on the spot, eh? I wonder if Collie knew that? He didn't mention it in his message."

And then he became aware of her pitiable condition.

"My dear young lady, where are you going to from here?" he asked kindly. "Did you drive yourself from Wimbledon?" And, when she nodded: "You certainly can't drive yourself back. You look all in!"

"I am all in," she smiled faintly, "and I most certainly do not feel like going to Wimbledon. Has anybody asked for me?"

There was no reason in the world why anybody should inquire at the *Post-Courier* for her: she realized the futility of her question.

"Can you tell me this?" she asked. "Have they caught the—the man who killed Mr. Sutton?"

She saw a peculiar look come to his face—something that was made up of consternation and penitence—then, dimly, she understood the cause. It was occurring to Field now for the first time that he was speaking to the widowed bride of the murdered man.

"I'm terribly sorry, Mrs. Sutton " he began in a fluster, but she cut him short.

"I'm not worried about that. I know it sounds brutal, but I really am not—hurt. Have they caught the man who killed him? And how was he—killed?"

"He was shot—Collie heard the explosion, if he didn't dream it. Somebody is suspected, and I should imagine the police are searching for him, but they haven't caught him."

"You mean—Captain Leslie?"

"That is the gentleman. Collie only passed it on as a rumour."

He himself was growing impatient: he had been too long away from his desk for his comfort. The press hour was approaching, and the fuller story of the night was yet to come from Collie.

"I think you ought to go back to Wimbledon. There are two or three reporters here who can drive a car. Would you let one of them take you back?"

She considered this.

"Yes, I think that will be wisest," she confessed. "I must be—somewhere where they can find me, mustn't I?"

He vanished to an upper region and returned with a red-haired youth.

"This chap lives at Wimbledon. You'll be doing him a turn if you let him drive you," he said.

She was grateful to the news editor for taking the decision out of her hands.

"I ought to have left the office hours ago," he told her as he accompanied her to the door. "But this is too big a story to leave to—"

He was evidently about to libel somebody, but changed his mind, and Beryl, who knew nothing about the internal policy of a newspaper office, shivered.

To this man, the supreme tragedy of the day was merely "a story." Her marriage, the death of her husband, the chase and capture of John Leslie... just a story; something that interested him and would be made even more interesting from day to day till the "story" died in the paragraph that described John Leslie's execution.

It aroused almost a feeling of revulsion toward the cheery youth who drove her through the wet night. Happily, he was not interested in murders: he chatted brightly on football till the car stopped under the portico of Hillford. She had hardly thanked the driver before the door opened.

"Is that you, miss?" It was Robert, the footman. "Mr. Friedman is back. I told him about your having gone to sleep and everything—and, miss, they telephoned from a newspaper, the *Megaphone*..."

She brushed past him and ran into the library. Lew Friedman was standing before the fireplace, his arms resting on the mantelpiece, his head on the back of his folded hands. At the sound of the opening door, he turned quickly, and she was startled at his appearance. His face had gone gray and old since she had seen him last.

He came stumbling toward her like a blind man and caught her in his arms.

"My dear, my dear!" he murmured brokenly. "Thank God, you're home again!"

"Lew!" She looked up into his face. "Do you know what has happened?"

He did not answer her.

"Frank Sutton is dead!" she whispered.

Still he stared past her.

"And, Lew, do you know who killed him?... I must tell you—all the newspapers will print it in the morning. John Leslie killed him!"

He dropped his head and looked at her from under his shaggy brows.

"John Leslie killed him? Who told you that?" he asked harshly.

She shook her head.

"Everybody knows it... I was there."

"At the Leopards Club?" he breathed.

"No, outside. I went there to find Mr. Collie, but when I arrived they had just discovered that—that the murder had been committed. Oh, Lew, it was horrible—horrible!"

"But who told you it was John Leslie?" he insisted.

"I heard her saying—Millie Trent. You remember, Lew, his secretary. She was screaming!" She screwed up her eyes in a grimace of pain. "I shall always hear her screaming."

"Where was she?"

"Being brought out of the club. She was crying that John Leslie had murdered Frank."

He put her away from him, held her at arms' length.

"Then she was screaming a lie," he said. "The man who killed him was not John Leslie—if it is necessary, I will go into the witness box to testify that he is innocent!"

239

CHAPTER XXX

SUTTON'S clerks had left. The night commissionaire was dozing in his box when John Leslie came walking quickly down the street, unlocked the main door of the building, and passed in. All the lights on the big stairway had been extinguished, except one electric bulb at an upper floor that gave sufficient light for the night watchman to make his rounds.

He went straight to his old room, inserted a key in the lock of his door, and then, finding it unfastened, entered the room and switched on the light. Rivulets of water were running from his long black raincoat, and this he took off and hung over the back of a chair, before he went to his desk. The sight of a key on the pad brought a frown to his face. Somebody had been here lately. He gave one glance at the fireplace, and the scattered embers told their own story. Who had been raking in the grate for evidence?

Curiously enough, he hit upon the right man at the first guess; for he had no small estimation of Mr. Joshua Collie's ability as a news gleaner. There was one little dossier, however, that was not disturbed. In the bottom drawer of his desk, which he had had fitted with a special lock, was a heavy steel box, which he lifted on to the table and unlocked. It contained so many papers that, when the lid was thrown up, two or three documents spilled to the blotting pad, He turned the box upside down, emptying it, and then, putting on the table lamp, he began a systematic examination of these scraps and pieces that he had collected during the period of his service.

Some of the notes that he examined were unintelligible, but two were tragedies in themselves: long parchment slips announcing the marriage, in one case of "Henry Whigton," in the other of "Rudolph Stahl," two of Mr. Frank Sutton's favourite aliases. He had been married in Capetown and in Bristol, which latter for some reason is the favourite rendezvous of English bigamists.

The second he studied for a long time. Mr. Rudolph Stahl had married Gwendoline Alice

The third name was familiar enough to him; it was his own, and the girl whose name had been written in the flowing hand of the registrar's clerk was his sister. He had been in France at the time, and had not met the bridegroom, nor did he know anything of the occurrence until he heard of the desertion, and learned from their uncle that half the girl's modest fortune had been assigned to the unknown Stahl.

Not as great a tragedy as it might have been, he thought with satisfaction as he folded up the marriage certificate. Hearts, especially young hearts, do not readily break, and after the inevitable divorce from the husband who was not the husband, she had married a barrister of New Zealand. And this little drama had been the incentive which put him on the track of The Squealer.

Among the papers was a small notebook that had been kept in shorthand—there was no doubting Millie Trent's qualifications for a secretaryship. It was not the ordinary shorthand of commerce, but one which had taken him months to decipher. This record of villainy covered many years.

The Squealer was a rich man: he had cached in a dozen banks the proceeds of his depredations. One of the documents was a cutting from an official police gazette, and this was interesting as supplying the only portrait that was in any way a likeness to Frank Sutton.

Wanted for bigamy and attempted murder, Jan Stefansson, believed to be a native of Sweden...

Here followed a description which contained many curious errors.

The vanity of criminals is proverbial, and there was no need to wonder why Sutton and his wife had preserved this damning piece of evidence; for at the end of the description of the man were the words:

Speaks several languages; is very good-looking and plausible, and a clever business man.

This little bit of flattery had led to the preservation of the notice.

He replaced the papers, locked the box, preparatory to taking it away (he would have carried it off that afternoon, but by some mischance had not recovered the keys that were taken from him when he was searched at the police station). He was taking a final look round when he heard the sound of footsteps in the passage. Whoever was the visitor, he or she was not well acquainted with the topography of the place, for now and again the footsteps ceased, and he could imagine the visitor peering at the inscriptions on the various doors. Presently, they came to a halt before his own room; the handle turned and the door opened slowly. It was Bill Anerley. He wore an overcoat buttoned to his chin, and beneath, the gold-laced trousers of his commissionaire's uniform looked a little ludicrous. He took off his cloth cap and shut the door behind him. It would appear that he had been running, for his breath came in gasps.

"Well, my friend?" Leslie was quietly amused.

Evidently Bill saw nothing humorous in the situation. His big mouth drooped pathetically, and there were tears in his eyes.

"I took a chance of finding you. One of the 'busies' told me you were working here," said Bill, speaking at a tremendous rate. And then he wailed: "What are you hanging about for, Captain: You ought to be getting along! This isn't the time to be sitting round in a place where everybody will come to look for you!

"So I think," said Leslie, a twinkle in his eye. "You mean they're coming after me? How did my name crop up?"

Bill shook his head in despair.

"That bird Millie. She's been shouting to the police. I slipped away—I was lucky. I sent down my boy to find a policeman, and before you could say 'knife' the club was full of 'em! I never knew there was so many coppers!"

He put his hand in his pocket and took out a roll of Treasury notes.

"Here you are, you'll want this—twenty-eight pounds: it's the day's takings."

He offered the money, but Leslie's hand did not move.

"Why, Percy," he said gently, "what's this?"

Bill's head drooped pathetically.

"I like to hear that word, sir." He pushed the money toward the other. "I wish it was hundreds. It'll get you out of the country."

Leslie pressed back the gift and shook his head.

"No, Percy, thank you, old boy." He dropped his hand on Bill's shoulder. "I've plenty of money—all the money I shall require at the moment."

Bill grunted his relief.

"Thank Gawd for that!" he said. "I don't mean I wouldn't give you all I had." And then, almost pleadingly: "Captain, don't go messing about here—that Millie's raising a squeal that'll get you into trouble before the night's out."

"Where is she?" asked Leslie, but here Bill could not help him.

"She went away first, an' then the police doctor come and they shifted the body to the hospital. Why, Gawd knows. I never seen a deader man. I'm not blaming you," he added hastily: "Don't think I am." Again his voice rose to a wail. "Captain, don't hang about. You ought to know better than to be sitting down here when you might be making tracks for Harwich or somewhere. What are you waiting for?"

Sitting down, Leslie was; he had dropped into the one armchair the apartment held, and was stretching himself luxuriously.

"I'm waiting for something to happen, Percy," he said pleasantly.

"They'll give you that," said Bill grimly. "Three clear Sundays after your trial! What's up?"

Leslie was on his feet, his head bent, listening. Somebody else was coming.

245

"It looks as if we were having a busy night. Go through there, Percy." He pointed to the door leading to the little anteroom. "As soon as they come in, slip!"

He held out his hand.

"Good luck, Captain!" Bill's voice was very husky.

"If you get to heaven before I do—" began Leslie.

"I'll tell 'em you're busy," said the man in a voice which was hardly above a whisper; and he had hardly gone out of the room before Leslie pulled open the door leading to the corridor.

The man who was standing there in the long raincoat greeted him with a sardonic grin.

"Well, Tillman, what do you want—have you come for your wages?"

Tillman looked round the room expectantly.

"Where's Miss Stedman?" he asked.

"At Wimbledon, I suppose," said Leslie. "I'll tell you where she isn't—she's not on her way to Scotland."

But Tillman shook his head.

"No, she left Wimbledon." He looked suspiciously at Leslie. "You haven't seen her?"

"Left Wimbledon?" John Leslie was astonished. "With whom? Who told you this?"

The man did not answer till he had seated himself on the desk. Evidently, he anticipated a long stay.

"She left the house with you," he said coolly. "At least, that is the story the servants told me. I have seen her since, and if she didn't leave with you, why was she outside the Leopards Club during the recent—shall I say, unfortunate happening?"

Leslie was all alert now.

"You don't really mean that? She hasn't been near the Leopards Club, has she?" he asked quickly, and when Tillman nodded: "How do you know?"

"I saw her there. I was on my way to the club to perform a certain duty, a little too late, as it proved, for the police whistles were blowing when I arrived on the scene. And then I saw Miss Stedman; in fact, I put her into her cab, though she may not be aware of that fact, before I went into the club to do my job of work."

Leslie drew a long breath.

"Now, may I respectfully ask you"—he was tensely polite—"what happened at Wimbledon that caused Miss Stedman to leave?"

Tillman threw out his hands.

"I wish I were sure! All I know is that, immediately after you left, they could not find Miss Stedman—or Mrs. Sutton—and the last that I saw of Friedman was when he was raging up and down the garden calling for his car, and breathing vengeance—on you, I presume."

"Naturally," said Leslie. "And then what happened?"

"That is all I know, until I saw the young lady at the Leopards. I've just come from there."

He said this with a meaning emphasis, and Leslie looked him straight in the face.

"I'm not interested in your comings and goings."

"Aren't you? I tell you, I was at the Leopards Club soon after the murder was committed."

"Oh?" said Leslie indifferently.

Tillman waited a moment.

"That doesn't interest you either?"

"Not very much," was the reply.

"Does it interest you to know that Frank Sutton was murdered?"

"Not greatly," was the cool response. "He was due for something of the sort."

Tillman nodded.

"I think you said that this morning."

John Leslie came slowly toward him, his hands in his pockets.

"Will you be kind enough to tell me who the hell you are?"

"That is immaterial," said Tillman with a little smile. "Who killed Sutton?"

Leslie shrugged.

"And that is for a coroner's jury to decide," he said. "Do you realize they pay coroners fifteen hundred pounds a year for the purpose of investigating such affairs? Would you take the bread out of their mouths by asking me to give in advance, with very little knowledge, a decision they can only reach by long and arduous investigations?"

Tillman laughed.

"You're a cool devil," he said.

"Have you any work to do?" asked Leslie politely.

"Yes—pretty big work."

"Don't let me keep you from it."

And then Tillman's eyes fell upon the man's hand. Right across the back a livid scar showed—the scar of his accident. But there was something else: a tiny red smear.

"What is that on your hand?" he asked.

Leslie looked carefully at the mark, wetted a handkerchief and rubbed it off.

"Blood. I knocked my hand. Are you thrilled?" he demanded, and Tillman's voice changed.

"You were in the club to-night. You were seen coming out of the staff entrance. Did you meet anybody you knew?"

Leslie laughed helplessly at this.

"I don't know why I should answer your damn silly questions. The only person I knew was Mr. Joshua Collie."

Tillman started.

"Collie?" incredulously. "Was he in the club?"

"He was."

"Inside when the murder was committed?" he asked.

"I suppose so. That seems to worry you."

For a moment Tillman lost his equanimity.

"Why should I worry about—" Here he stopped.

"A reporter," said Leslie. "I know what's rattling you, my friend, Sutton was not sufficiently curious to ask for information about you when he took you on. I was. I have a curiosity complex."

Tillman had recovered his self-possession.

"Frank Sutton is dead," he said. "He was only married to-day—"

"He's only been married several days, but that doesn't matter. What do you want?" demanded Leslie. "You had better go home, my friend. You'll do no good here."

He opened the door.

"The servant said that Mrs. Sutton went away after you to-night," said Tillman, "and he told the truth—"

"Good-night," said Leslie.

"I shall be seeing you again, I think," said the disconcerted Tillman.

"I hope not," replied Leslie.

The sound of Tillman's footsteps had hardly died away before the third interruption came. He recognized instantly the patter of those quick feet, and with an exclamation ran to the door and threw it open. Beryl fell into his arms.

"Oh, Jack! Jack, my dear!" she breathed.

"Where have you come from?" he asked quickly.

"I've come from Wimbledon—no, not alone—Lew is outside in the car. He said he'd come up if you want to see him."

"Lew is outside in the car?" he repeated, and then: "You were at the Leopards Club to-night. You know?"

"About Frank? Yes. Is it true, John, he's dead?"

He nodded.

"Yes, Sutton is dead. My dear, I'm terribly sorry for you."

She was trying to nerve herself to ask a question. He saw her lips move and helped her.

"You're going to ask me where I was—when he was shot?"

She nodded.

"You didn't—you didn't—oh, Jack, answer me—who killed him?"

John Leslie did not meet her eyes lest she read the truth.

CHAPTER XXXI

"WHOEVER killed him, he deserved death," he said sternly. "The gallows was waiting for the murderer of poor Larry Graeme. Beryl, darling, this isn't making it easy for me to tell you. And I want to tell you—the truth. Sit down, my dear. You look worn out. Why did you leave Friedman's house this evening? They say you came after me?"

"I didn't, I didn't!" she said impatiently. "I went up to my dressing room and fell asleep. Lew looked for me and couldn't find me. He didn't think I'd gone after you. He thought I knew about Frank Sutton and had run away. Then, when I woke up, everybody was gone, and only then I came up to find—to find you. Tell me about what you were going to tell me—"

"I want to know why you came up to find me?" He sat on one arm of the chair into which he had forced her, and his arm was about her.

"I was just mad, I suppose," she said.

"The thought of not seeing you again. I went to the boarding house where you live, and then I went on to the newspaper, the *Post-Courier*. They thought you might be at the Leopards Club, so I drove there."

She shuddered.

"Poor darling!" he said, as he held her tightly. "I wish—but wishes aren't much use, are they?"

"But you didn't do it?" She was half hysterical. "Lew swears you are innocent. You didn't shoot him—you couldn't kill a man in cold blood, John?"

"Hush!" he said. "You shouldn't be here, darling. I'm going to take you down to Friedman. He ought not to have allowed you to come."

And then, with infinite tenderness in his voice:

"You're a dear girl. I wanted to save you from such a lot."

But she was insistent.

"You couldn't do it! I know you didn't! If you did, there must be some horrible reason."

He nodded slowly.

"There were horrible reasons why Sutton should die. I don't want to talk about them. Everything I've done has been wasted effort. I wanted to keep your name clean—and save you from humiliation. I'd have done it if—if he hadn't married you to-day."

She drew herself from his arms and stood up, and never had she seemed more forlorn than at that moment when she made her last heroic effort to appear indifferent to the tragedy of the night.

"I'm awfully sensible now—really. What are you going to do? You shouldn't be here another minute. Have you any money?"

"Everybody wants to give me money," he smiled. "Even old Percy."

"Percy?"

"You don't know him. His name is Anerley—an old soldier: I met him in France."

"Does he know?"

"He guesses." And then, with a sudden agitation which amazed her: "I wish I could tell you—I'm a fool! I'm a fool! And I've tried to be so clever! Yes, he knows—or thinks he knows. He's the porter at the Leopards Club. Poor old Percy!"

"Poor old Percy,'" she said, with a despairing smile. "Can't you think about yourself?"

"I do."

Somebody else had come into the corridor.

They had tracked him there, she thought, and at the sound of the new footsteps she went white.

"It isn't the police?" she asked.

"Get into that room"—he pointed to the way Anerley had gone—" and either make your escape from the building and return to Lew, or stay there quietly."

He slipped to the door, turned the key in the lock, and pushed home the bolt, only just in time, for the door handle rattled, and a shrill, vengeful voice, incoherent with fury, called him by name.

"It's Millie Trent," he whispered.

Stooping, he kissed her, and pointed. He waited until she was gone, and then he drew back the bolt, and Millie Trent almost fell into the room. Her hair was in disorder, her big eyes seemed an unnatural size in her colourless face. She stood, pointing a shaking finger at him, inarticulate with mad fury.

"You coward! You beast! You murderer!" she cried in a strangled voice.

She wore no coat; her blouse was shining with rain, her gray silk stockings bespattered with mud.

"Well?" His voice was hard and dry, and his very coolness made her coherent.

"Murderer—beast! You killed him! You said you would—you shot him! You couldn't stand up to him, but you shot him like a dog!"

"A mad dog," he said sternly. "He was nothing better, was he?"

Twice she opened her mouth to speak, and then, with a howl, she dragged apart the clasp of her bag, but before she could point the revolver, he had gripped her by the wrist and flung it clear.

"You dirty coward!" she whimpered. "But I'll see you on the scaffold for it! I'll have you hanged! I'll go to the police—Barrabal will get you! I'm not afraid of you, you butcher! I've brought somebody with me who is going to put your name in mud!"

"Be quiet." He thrust her down into a chair, and for a moment she was too exhausted to rise. "What sort of a woman are you?" he demanded hardly. "You've been stealing with him for years! You've been in every swindle with him— you've stood by and seen young hearts broken and young lives ruined—Mrs. Sutton!"

"It's a lie! He never went away with any of them! Do you think I'd stand for that? Mrs. Sutton! You knew, did you?"

He nodded.

"I tried to make you admit it in this office this very morning. I insulted you till you were on the point of telling me."

She leaped suddenly from the chair and ran to the door, dragging it open.

"I'm going to the police to tell them where you are!" she screamed. "They're looking for you—you know that, don't you?"

"They'll be looking for you too," he said.

She came back to him, thrust her face into his.

"Do you think I care what happens to me? They're going to get you, Leslie! I can look after myself. I don't want any help, you thieving convict—you butcher! Oh, God, I hate you! But I'll get you!"

Leslie picked up the pistol from the floor where he had thrown it and put it down on the desk.

"Is this the gun that your husband used to shoot Larry Graeme?" he asked.

"He shot him in self-defence," she raged. "Didn't they find a loaded gun on Graeme? Wasn't it in his hand when my man got him? Yes, he shot him—he'd have killed you if he'd known—if I die for it, I'll get you, Leslie. You murdered Frank—"

"That's not true."

It was Beryl: she had come silently into the room and confronted the mad woman.

"Oh, you're with him, are you? I might have expected that."

"I've been with him all the evening," said Beryl.

"You were at the Leopards Club with him, were you?" sneered Millie Trent, and before Beryl could answer, John Leslie spoke.

"No, she was not with me at the Leopards Club," he said quietly, and she looked at Beryl with a grin of hate.

"He wouldn't bring his little sweetie's name into the case, would he! But he's going to—if there's any mud, you'll get it, Beryl Sutton."

"It's mud enough to have that name," said Beryl.

257

"It was good enough for me," said Millie, with tragic inconsequence.

"Why didn't you use it?" demanded the man sternly. "Because you were out for any dirty graft that brought you money—don't interrupt me," he said, as she tried to speak. "There are men in half the convict prisons of England who were sent there by you and your husband. The last man who had my job is serving five years' penal servitude because he got a little too curious about Sutton's business. He didn't know that Sutton sent him to the Moor—that Sutton was The Squealer and that you sent the squeal! If Sutton were dead ten times over, he wouldn't have paid for all the misery he has brought to the men and women he has sacrificed."

"You murdered him!" she whimpered. "That's all I know—I'll get you."

"Get me," he said suddenly. "Go out and find a policeman and bring him in."

He slammed the door behind her and turned to the girl.

"Are you mad?" she breathed. "You are mad. You've got to get away. Don't you realize..."

"I want to see the somebody who came with her, and I've an idea that I know who that somebody is."

He opened the door and looked along the ill-lighted corridor. A few paces away Mr. Joshua Collie was leaning against the wall with an expression of utter weariness, a sad-looking cigarette drooping from his lips.

CHAPTER XXXII

"COME in, Collie. Did you bring that nice young lady here?"

"She brought me," said Mr. Collie sadly. "She is rather a masterful woman. Most women are masterful." Here he saw Beryl and bowed. "I'm afraid I'm rather unexpected and a little *de trop.*"

"You're always unexpected, Mr. Collie," said Leslie, and Joshua smiled, as though he had received a great compliment.

"Ubique is my middle name," he said, and then shook his head. "Poor little girl! I'm thinking, at the moment," he added hastily, "of that unfortunate woman who left this room a few seconds ago."

He looked at his rain-sodden coat and seemed to find the spectacle interesting.

"It's a remarkable fact that interesting murders are generally committed on rainy nights, when taxicabs cannot be hired for love or money. I remember it was such a night when Crippen murdered his wife and buried her in a coal cellar." He smiled broadly. "It was rather an amusing case— in some ways. And, by the way, they've shut the club."

"The Leopards?"

Collie nodded.

"It was rather an arbitrary action on the part of the police. Fortunately," he said, "they shut the bar last. But that was because I was there with the inspector in charge of the case. A very nice fellow who only drinks tonic water."

"You were there when—er—"

"When—er," repeated Collie. "Shall I call it a tragedy occurred? I was an eyewitness."

John Leslie took a step backward and the girl thought his face changed colour.

"I was an eyewitness, and yet I was not an eyewitness," said Joshua, his eyes fixed upon Leslie. "I saw somebody fire a shot, and yet I will not swear that I could recognize the person who fired that shot. Then again," he went on in his exasperating fashion, "suppose one did recognize him, and he stood his trial for murder, what consequences would follow? I am not a lawyer, but what I ask you is what would happen, supposing one kills a murderer, or suppose one shoots in self-defence? That is an hypothesis which Miss Trent produced on our way here. I rather gathered that she was trying to excuse the killing of Larry Graeme. But such questions are not to be answered by a mere newspaper reporter, brilliant, painstaking and conscientious as he undoubtedly is."

"There's one question I'd like to ask you, Collie—does Miss Stedman's name go into this?"

"Miss Stedman's name cannot be kept out of this—now!"

"But the narrative so far as she is concerned should end with the wedding?"

Joshua nodded.

"In my story, it undoubtedly ends with the wedding, Mr. Leslie. But will her connection end there in the police story?"

There was a pause.

"Tillman saw her," said Leslie.

"Tillman!" Joshua Collie said this so shrilly that for a moment Leslie had an idea that he was singing. "Was Tillman there?"

"He was outside the Leopards Club. He saw Miss Stedman."

"Outside, you say? And he saw Miss Stedman? Humph! That's unfortunate. You're sure he was outside? You didn't see him yourself or speak to him?" he asked eagerly.

Leslie could reassure him on that point.

"It is very unfortunate. The last thing in the world I could wish to have happened."

Collie was speaking as though the tragedy had been staged by himself.

"I have never known anything more unfortunate."

Then, apropos of nothing, Leslie said brusquely to the girl: "Down you come to your car, and so home to Wimbledon."

"But, dear—" she began.

262

"I insist. I want to be alone, as I shall be after leaving you at Wimbledon, to think things over. And I want to see Mr. Collie again to-night—and particularly do I wish to see Mr. Tillman," he added grimly. "I rather think Mr. Tillman is going to be difficult."

"He is an extremely nice man," interrupted Joshua. "I am not referring to him in a professional capacity, but as a human being. Nor would I say he was one of nature's noblemen. But he is a really nice man, considering."

"That we shall discover," said Leslie.

Lew Friedman sat huddled up in a corner of the car, and hardly spoke a word all the way back to Wimbledon. He did no more than give Leslie a gruff greeting, nor did he speak to the girl, being content to hold her hand throughout the journey. Leslie tried to make conversation, but with no conspicuous success.

He was heartily glad when Hillford was reached.

In the atmosphere of his own home, Lew Friedman became more like his natural self. He had been terribly shaken by the events of the evening, and for the first time Beryl saw and realized how old he was.

"Are you coming into the library, or are you going up to your room to sleep?"

She shook her head.

"I've been to sleep, Lew," she said quietly. "I don't know whether I wish I hadn't."

263

"Thank God you did!" said the man gruffly.

He pushed open the door of the library, and they went in. No word was spoken till Robert appeared with a tray of steaming hot coffee and a large decanter. Lew poured himself out a stiff dose and drank it quickly.

"That's good," he said as he dropped into his old chair and spread out his shaking hands to the dying embers. "God! what a night!"

"You know, Lew—don't you?"

"About Sutton? Yes, I know all about that." He jerked his head round to Leslie. "Did you tell her?"

"I told her Sutton was dead."

"Did you tell her that he was—what he was?"

"No," said Leslie.

Beryl was looking at him in surprise.

"What he was? But I don't understand."

"He was The Squealer," said Lew harshly; "and he was something else, Beryl, my girl—you remember one night we were talking about a man in this very room who had made a hobby of bigamy?"

She nodded at this.

"Yes, you said burglary was clean, and I wondered why you said it. And then you told us about this horrible man. Oh!" she gasped. "It wasn't—"

"Frank Sutton," said Lew. "When I heard—I thought I should go mad!"

"How did you know, Friedman?" asked Leslie.

It had puzzled him all the evening as to how the information had come to Lew Friedman.

"I heard some voices in the drawing room," said Lew. "To tell you the truth, I was a little suspicious about certain little exchanges I had witnessed between Sutton and the girl Trent. And then I heard them, as I thought, quarrelling. I was a little worried, and in ordinary circumstances of course I had never dreamed of listening. But I had you to think of, Beryl." He took her hand in his and crushed it until she winced. "I had your happiness, your future to consider, and I was taking no chances. I had to know just what this woman was to him, and I turned the handle of the door, opened it a little—and then I heard the whole foul story! I'd married my girl to The Squealer, a fence, a receiver of stolen goods, and worse than that—he was already married. He'd left the other women at the church door."

His voice shook.

"But he wasn't going to leave you. I think I must have gone mad then, and the wonder is I didn't rush in and strangle him. I wish I had now. But it was you, and the thought of you upstairs, unaware of the dreadful thing that had happened, that steadied me. I went up to see you to tell you, not only to tell you but to get a little balance from you, darling. Do you remember when I used to have those fits of anger how I came to you to be cooled off? Well, I went back to the old way. When I got to your room I couldn't find you. If I'd been sane I'd have knocked at the door of your dressing room. Then I got a mad idea that you knew all about Sutton and had run away.

When a man's unbalanced, he gets those kind of stupid notions. I dashed into my room and changed my clothes—I was still wearing the falderals that I'd worn for the wedding. For a moment, in my anxiety for you, I forgot all about Sutton. When I got downstairs, he'd gone. I knew where I should find him, so I got the car and went up to town to look for him. I didn't dream of going to the office; if I had, I'd have found him there, as it happened. Instead, I went somewhere else."

Now she understood, and rose to her feet, looking down at him, her eyes wide with horror.

"You went to the Leopards Club?" she said. He nodded.

"I went to the Leopards Club, yes. You see, I know Anerley, and once, when he was very, very hard up, I helped him because he was an old soldier. I met him originally at the Cape during the war. I hadn't been there for years, but decided to go to-night."

"You were, in fact, the sleeping gentleman in Number Four?" said Leslie with a smile.

Lew nodded.

"I only had one idea in my head—to settle with Frank Sutton. Nobody saw me come into the club except Anerley. His boy was out at the time. Naturally, he was surprised to see me. I told him I wasn't feeling up to the mark and wanted to sleep, and that I didn't wish anybody to know that I was there. I had to take the chance of getting a room near the one Sutton would take. As it happened, he gave me the one next to the board room. I heard Sutton come in and, by listening at the thin partition wall, I heard his conversation on the telephone. I opened the door, and then he saw me; he jumped to his feet, pulled his gun, and I fired."

"You killed him? It was you—you?" she breathed. Beryl looked at him with wide eyes. "You—you!" she whispered again. "You killed him, Lew?"

He nodded slowly. His head dropped forward on his breast.

"I killed him. I'm not ashamed of it. I'll stand my trial for it. If ever a man deserved death, it was he."

She looked wildly at Leslie.

"You knew, then, all the time?"

"He knew," broke in Lew. "Just as I fired, I felt somebody strike up my arm, and I looked round—it was Leslie. He took the pistol from my hand and pushed me through the door of a little service staircase that leads to the ground floor; the waiters use it. I didn't meet anybody. I had to unbar the door when I got to the bottom. It is opened and closed by Anerley himself."

"Oh, Lew!"

She was on her knees by his side, his big hand between hers, her head resting against his arm, and she was sobbing and laughing like someone demented.

It was a long time before they could calm her, and by the time she had recovered, Leslie was gone.

"He's off to see Tillman," explained Lew.

"But Tillman?" She was bewildered. "Who is he? What is he?"

But here he was unable to satisfy her.

He himself had a duty to perform, and he waited till the doctor he had summoned had come and gone before he sent for his weary chauffeur.

"I want you to take me to Bow Street police station," he said. "I shall not be returning. You will bring the car back to Wimbledon and hold yourself at Miss Beryl's orders."

He spent half an hour putting his affairs in order, then getting in the car, he was driven rapidly back to town. He was hardly out of the house before the telephone bell rang furiously.

The half-hour after midnight was striking when the mud-covered car drew up before the dingy portals of Bow Street police station. Lew Friedman lingered a little while in the rain to give final instructions.

"No, you needn't wait to pick me up," he said, with a certain grim humour. "In fact, it may be a very long time before you pick me up again, Jones. See Captain Leslie in the morning, and he will probably help you to make up your mind whether you will stay in my employ or not."

He did not move till the car had driven off, and then, mounting the four steps, he walked up to the constable at the door.

"I want to see the inspector in charge," he said, and the officer led him into the brightly lighted charge room.

As it happened, both the uniformed and the detective inspector were at that moment at the desk talking to the station sergeant.

"My name is Lewis Friedman," he said.

"I know you very well, Mr. Friedman." smiled the inspector. "What can we do for you? Have you lost?"

"I've come to give myself up on a charge of murder," said Lew Friedman steadily. "At about nine-thirty to-night I shot and killed a man who is known as Frank Sutton, but who is probably better known to you as The Squealer. I killed him at the Leopards Club."

The detective inspector was gazing at him in amazement.

"Not guilty," he said, and then suddenly he laughed. "I'm afraid, Mr. Friedman," he said, "you've been looking on the wine when it was red!"

"I tell you I killed him," said Lew impatiently.

The inspector shook his head.

"I can assure you that you didn't," he said. "I've just come from the Middlesex Hospital, where Sutton, whose other name is Stahl, is lying, and he is not even wounded."

Lew could not believe his ears. He passed his hand across his eyes in bewilderment. Sutton was alive....?

"I'm not dreaming this?" he said huskily. "If he isn't... shot, why is he in hospital?"

"He is in hospital," said the detective, "because, according to his own statement, having prepared a knock-out drop with which he intended to put a lady friend to sleep, he inadvertently drank it himself. In other words he is merely suffering from narcotic poisoning; and if half the squeal of his lady friend is true, he ought to be well enough to hang in six weeks."

CHAPTER XXXIII

MR. FIELD should have left his office at the latest by six o'clock. It is true that newspaper men keep no rigid times, and that the exigencies of their peculiar profession frequently detain them hours after they should be in the bosom of their families. But news editors as a rule are men of habit, train catchers, who would leave their office in the middle of an earthquake at the dictation of a time-table. And here it was one o'clock in the morning, and Mr. Field was sitting on a table in his shirt-sleeves, the butt of a cigar between his teeth, and, behind those shining spectacles of his, a look of satisfaction in his tired eyes.

He had before him a copy of the *Megaphone*, wet from the press, and how he had obtained this early specimen of a rival sheet was known only to Mr. Field and his Maker. Before him, seated in Mr. Field's sacred writing chair, lounged Joshua Collie; and in front of him a large paper of ham sandwiches and a long glass half filled with beer.

"There are wonderful experiences for a man in life, Collie," said Field, who at one o'clock in the morning was prone to grow a trifle didactic. "There is, for example, the first act of encouragement you receive from a pretty girl—"

"I have never received any act of encouragement from any pretty girl," protested Joshua through a ham sandwich.

"I am not referring to you, but to more attractive men," said Mr. Field; "and there is, I should imagine, the joy that comes to a warrior's heart when he has vanquished his enemy."

Mr. Field took a sip of his own refreshment and put down the glass.

"But there is no thrill quite like reading the paper across the road."

"Round the corner," suggested Collie, who had a passion for exactness.

"Or even round the corner. And we have beaten them—"

"I have beaten them," murmured Collie.

"You are one of the mass for the moment. If you hadn't been spurred and kicked and insulted from your natural inertia, you would never have got this story. And I'll be handsome with you, Collie. You've picked up The Squealer threads quicker than any other man in Fleet Street could have picked them up. This rag"—he tapped the unoffending *Megaphone*—"has had its best man on the job for weeks. You snooped in under his nose and you lammed the life out of him. And the crowning—" He paused for a word.

"Triumph," suggested Joshua.

"'Achievement' is the word I was trying to find. Your crowning achievement was the discovery that The Squealer is still alive. That I regard as your *tour de force*"

"Or *chef d'oeuvre*" murmured Joshua.

The telephone bell on the table buzzed. Field reached round lazily and picked it up.

"I'm not interested in anything now," he said, "except bed."

It was the hall porter speaking, and as he listened Field's grin broadened.

"Well, if that doesn't beat everything!" he said, in an awe-stricken voice. "Ask him to come up."

He replaced the receiver and looked at Collie.

"A friend of yours wishes to congratulate you."

Mr. Collie was not tremendously interested in the congratulations of his friends. He too was feeling the strain; and when the swing doors were opened and "Tillman" came in, a broad grin on his saturnine face, he rose to meet his generous rival; for Arthur Tillman Jones of the *Megaphone* had for years been regarded as the greatest crime reporter in Fleet Street.

"I take off my hat to you, you old clue-hound!" he said, as he gripped Joshua's hands. "I've just purloined one of your early editions."

And as Field vainly attempted to conceal the copy of the *Megaphone*:

"You're not the only corrupt influence in Fleet Street, Field. And your story's great, Collie—truly great. We shall have to come out with a later edition and pinch as much as we can from you, but you've got a start on us in the country that will do us no good at all. By the way, have you seen our friend Leslie?"

Mr. Collie looked up at the clock.

"He swore he'd call before he went home," he said. "That's why I'm waiting. Marvellous chap! He got that job with The Squealer because of his bad character—Sutton only wanted old lags about him; so Leslie obliged him. Scotland Yard faked his previous convictions."

"Why didn't that fool sergeant from Marylebone know him?" asked Tillman Jones.

"Who does know him? Of course, as soon as he got inside and told the inspector who he was, Elford got him out."

"Who he was—" began Tillman Jones.

Leslie came in at that moment, unannounced. He had the trick of passing janitors and guards without so much as "by your leave." As he strode into the room, he flung out his hand to Collie.

"Congratulations! It reads true even if it isn't true!"

Joshua was one huge smile, and then he turned to Field.

"Mr. Field," he said, "I'd like you to meet Chief Inspector Barrabal of Scotland Yard."

Two hands gripped over the news editor's desk.

"How do you do!" said Field.

"How do you do!" said John Leslie Barrabal.

THE END